An

Ex-Heiress

in

Emeralds

An
Ex-Heiress
in
Emeralds

A Gemstone Mystery

Mary E. Stibal

LEVEL
BEST BOOKS

Library of Congress Control Number: 2021943912

PHOTO CREDIT: Photo by Lori A. Magno

First edition

ISBN: 978-1-953789-63-1

Cover art by Level Best Designs

This book was professionally typeset on Reedsy.
Find out more at reedsy.com

I dedicate this book to my beloved sisters and brothers, Sharon, Mike, Tom, John, Judy, Jim, Bill, Theresa, Ann, and Marlene. All of them, oddly enough, on the bossy side. Opinionated too.

The Word on the Street

"If you love Boston and drop-dead jewelry, and if murder mysteries are up your alley, The Gemstone Mysteries is a 'can't put it down' new series!"
—Mary Buckham, *USA Today* Bestselling Author

Chapter One

MILTON, MASSACHUSETTS

C ool eyes scanned the gleaming rows of military-grade weapons in the gun room, all legal, all high-end, but worthless. There was a deer hunting rifle in here, somewhere. Walking quickly, the figure went up and down the two aisles. Finally, in the back of the long room there it was, a powerful Browning X-Bolt, one of the best rifles for bringing down a big buck.

Although a deer wasn't the target.

Gloved hands picked up the rifle and expertly checked the bolt. Yes, this would be perfect.

BOSTON, MASSACHUSETTS

Coda Gems

Some of the customers who walked into Coda Gems on Boston's Newbury Street had serious money, the eight-figure kind. The rest were simply rich. Which made Madeline Lane, co-owner of the upscale gem and jewelry store, happy.

Most of the time.

Unfortunately, there were those customers who grated on her nerves, like the one on Tuesday morning. The slender, mid-30's woman, in a gray cashmere jacket and slacks ignored Madeline when she set yet another 18 karat gold bracelet in front of her. The seventeenth one so far, or maybe it was the eighteenth. The woman picked up the bracelet, set it back on the glass counter, and without a word grabbed her handbag and headed to the door.

Madeline watched her walk away and muttered, "Do you have to leave so soon? I was just about to poison the tea."

As the glass door of Coda Gems swung shut behind the woman, Madeline ran her fingers through her curly blonde hair. Around her neck was a gold jeweler's loupe that she wore every day, like a necklace. She turned to Abby, her business partner, who'd walked up beside her and said, "Well good riddance to that one."

Abby replied, frowning, "And thanks to you, it's probably permanent. I heard what you said. I'm not deaf and it's likely she isn't either."

"Well, she was rude. Who does she think she is?"

"A potential customer. But not anymore," said Abby. Her hair was a short glossy black, and her suit, 100% natural fibers, was a shade of blue. She had at least seven.

"Let me tell you about the very rich," said Madeline. "They are different from you and me."

"Well, that's your opinion."

"That's not an opinion, that's a quote. F. Scott Fitzgerald."

"Whatever, Madeline. Your attitude can sometimes be…unhelpful. You've got to watch what you say. I'm serious."

Madeline rolled her eyes. Five months before Coda Gems had moved from the bustle of gritty downtown Boston to the exclusive and expensive Newbury Street fifteen blocks away. A move that was a financial gamble for Coda, as well as a big change. Abby was thrilled, Madeline not so much. Some of their new customers were, no other way to describe them, insufferable.

The two partners glared at each other in icy silence. They'd worked out their roles when they'd started their upscale jewelry business three years before; Abby was the primary salesperson and the de facto CFO, while Madeline was the store's buyer, handling estate and online jewelry auctions, as well as buying from Boston and New York gem dealers. She worked with customers too of course, when she was in the store. However, she could be outspoken, which Abby had pointed out more than once the rich didn't always appreciate.

Madeline yanked open the back of the front glass case, slid the unwanted Tiffany and Cartier bracelets inside, and said over her shoulder, "Some of these customers think their money means they are... superior."

"I wouldn't go that far."

"Well, I would. Actually, I just did."

Abby just shook her head, "Madeline, maybe the problem is that you are just too sensitive," she said. "Toughen up, and let what they say or do just slide," and she stormed up the steps to her desk in the open loft in the back.

* * *

Ten minutes later a young couple walked in the door and strolled along their jewelry cases as Abby walked up to them. "Good morning. Can I help you?"

A third customer came in and Madeline was showing him their ruby jewelry, but then Abby took a call on her cell, and walking over, whispered to Madeline, "Sorry, can you take over for me?" She nodded to the couple, "They're looking for a birthday present for his mother. Something sapphire." Abby didn't wait for a response, but went back into the office. She came out thirty minutes later, her face pale.

"What's up?" said Madeline as she set a sapphire and diamond brooch back in the glass case.

Abby shook her head, her black hair falling over her brown eyes tight with worry. "That was my Dad. Mom...Mom is in the ICU at the University of Chicago hospital. She had a heart attack this morning."

"Oh my God Abby. How is she?" Madeline turned the lock in the case and walked up to her.

"She's stable now, and they're running tests." Abby sighed, "Anyway, I booked a flight to Chicago that leaves in two hours, so I have to run home and pack."

"Of course, yes, you must go right away. I'll be fine running Coda, and I'll…"

"Well, Madeline, I've been thinking about that. Someone should be here, to…to help you. I mean with customers. You know, maybe Martin could come in while I'm gone? After all, he does know our inventory, and he might be willing to help us out. We'll pay for his gas, and commute time too."

Martin was a jeweler who used to manage the store for them on Sundays and had usually been available whenever they needed backup. But he'd moved to Duxbury on the South Shore three months before, almost an hour away.

"Martin? Not him, definitely no. Don't worry, I'll be just fine," and she hugged Abby. "Retail is slow now, since it's the beginning of November after all, and besides, there aren't any estate auctions or gem shows coming up, so I can be here full time. By myself."

Abby said nothing, she just stared at Madeline, and after a long, uncomfortable minute that stretched into a second one, Madeline sighed and said, "Fine then, I'll see if Martin can come in. He might be busy, but I'll check. Anyway, you need to go. Call me later, and don't worry about the store."

Abby clasped and unclasped her hands, then glanced around the store. "Thanks, it's just that you…" her voice trailing off. "Yes, I should leave." And she left for her car in the garage down the block.

Madeline did call Martin an hour later, but unfortunately, he was neither busy nor out-of-town. He could be there at noon the next day. To be honest, the man drove her crazy.

He all but genuflected when a customer radiating big money walked in the door.

* * *

That evening Madeline's cell phone was ringing as she walked in the door of her condo building in the Seaport District. She grabbed her phone, glancing at the caller ID. It was Felix, and she let his call go to voicemail. She worried that Abby hadn't called, and then she did.

"I'm here, at the hospital. Mom is out of the woods thank God. She was just moved to a regular room, and she can go home in two or three days. Which is wonderful."

"Abby, I am so glad. you must be relieved. That is very good news."

"Thanks, and yes, it is. Still, my Mom is a bit shaky, so I'm going to stay in Chicago for at least a week."

"No problem. By the way, I called Martin. He'll be here tomorrow afternoon, and he can come in every day this week."

She heard Abby give a big sigh of relief, which Madeline thought was overly dramatic. And annoying.

* * *

Madeline walked into Coda Gems at 8:00 a.m. the next morning. She was always at the store at least an hour before they opened, she liked the extra time to get ready for the day. As usual, she was in black designer jeans and hand-tooled cowboy boots. Todays were a delicate, pale orange. It was fall after all, and she was nothing if not seasonal.

As she took their jewelry out of the safe and set up the displays in their glass cases, she wished Martin wasn't coming in. It would just be easier to be alone in the store until Abby came back.

She and Abby were a bit of an odd couple as far as business partners go. Abby was a 'by-the-book type,' Madeline not so much, in point of fact, not at all. What made it work was they were both devoted to their fledgling business and managed to smooth over their differences. Mostly.

Madeline made a cup of coffee and critically eyed their store. They'd bought new furniture when they'd moved to their new location; the sofa, as well as the matching bar stools scattered around the cut-glass counters, were a rich brown leather, and on the walls hung prints of Boston Symphony seasons from the 1930s in matte black frames. Which Madeline thought gave their store a hush of 'Old Money,' even though they were barely breaking even.

So far.

5

At noon Martin walked in the door, still tall and thin, wearing a pale gray suit, his dark hair slicked back, and his shoes black patent leather. He looked like a man who might break into a foxtrot at any moment.

"It's good to be back," he said, smiling. His oversize blue glasses were new. Madeline couldn't take her eyes off them. He set his bulky umbrella, in the closet. She'd forgotten about that, Martin was never without his umbrella. "I like to be prepared," he had said once when she'd commented on it. Obviously, even when the temperature was below freezing.

Only a few customers came in, and she let Martin handle them since she was behind on her appraisals for three clients. But when she overheard him tell a customer in head-to-toe Versace, who'd asked to see a very ordinary, run-of-the-mill diamond bracelet, "Excellent, excellent choice. I do have to admire your good taste," Madeline all but ground her teeth.

She couldn't bear the thought of listening to him every day for a week.

Then at 3:00, Martin announced, "I just checked the weather, and I'm sorry, but I have to beat a big snow storm heading straight for Duxbury. I think I should leave right away. I hope you don't mind."

Madeline smiled, "Of course you should definitely leave for home," and she was relieved when he left.

Three hours later, thank God, she read an alert on her computer that the storm had shifted directions and was forecast to move north to Boston late that night, so she called Martin. "It's going to be bad here tonight, up to eleven inches of snow," she said. "So don't bother to try and come in. I'll pay you of course for the day. Why don't I check in with you tomorrow afternoon about the rest of the week?"

"You're sure?" he asked.

"Martin, I am most definitely, absolutely sure."

She would call him the next day, and come up with a good reason for him not to come in again. She'd be just fine by herself.

On her way home after she'd closed the store her cell phone rang. The caller ID said 'Felix'. She didn't pick up this time either.

* * *

The next morning Madeline was waiting on a young couple buying wedding rings when a heavy-set man in his mid-50's, with thick, dark eyebrows and streaks of silver in his brown hair walked in, with a man in his late 20's wearing an expensive gray suit, who said to the older man, "Here? This place? But Dad, we're already running late. We can find a better..."

"Don't worry about it. I need to see something," the older man looked over at Madeline, "Clerk, I want to see the watch in the window. The Patek."

Madeline told the couple she'd be just a moment and took the sterling silver watch out of the window. She explained to the man, "Each Patek Philippe watch, Swiss-made, is hand-finished, and..."

"Spare me, I know all about them. I collect Patek's." He pulled up his sleeve, to show a heavy, 18 karat-gold Patek timepiece on his wrist. He held out his hand for the silver watch, but instead, Madeline set it in front of him on a black velvet pad. Without a word he picked it up, turned it over, and inspected the back.

He said, "Well, at least it's real, on the low end, but real. Still, even a low-end Patek is better than any other watch, at any price." His eyes swept across their jewelry cases and he turned toward her, his dark eyes piercing. "I see you have emerald jewelry."

"Yes, I just brought in a new emerald collection, Columbian of course. They are gorgeous. I can..."

"Never mind, I doubt you'll have what I'm looking for," and he signaled to his son studying their Boston Symphony posters and the two men walked out the door.

Madeline was glad they'd left.

But the man was back, three hours later, alone this time.

"Hello again. How can I help you?" said Madeline.

The man didn't respond, just walked over to their case of emerald jewelry, so she went back to re-arranging the diamond bracelets.

Then he turned toward her, "Clerk?"

She walked over, "The name is Lane. Madeline Lane." She was being funny. Sort of. The man either missed the James Bond reference or ignored it.

"Whatever. I want to buy my wife an emerald necklace. A first-anniversary

7

present, so it needs to be spectacular." And he drummed his fingers on the glass counter. "What else do you have?"

She took a Bulgari gold necklace with four carats of emeralds out of a drawer and set it on a black velvet pad on the counter, but he waved his hand airily, "I said 'spectacular'. That one is not 'spectacular'."

Madeline hesitated, then set the necklace back in the drawer. "I see. Well, tell me more about what you're looking for, and if we don't have it, I can have a piece or two sent in for you to consider."

"I need a necklace, an emerald necklace, at least ten or twelve carats. In four days. Got that? And I want the best. I've been to Tiffany, but they don't understand the meaning of 'right away.' So can you find something I'll want to buy in four days, or is this conversation a waste of my time?" He checked his watch and looked up at her, impatiently. "Just say yes or no."

She stared at him, not about to answer. The man was a jerk.

He glanced at their glass cases again, and then back to her. "I've checked out emerald necklaces online you know, so don't jack up the price on me."

Madeline said, an edge in her voice, "Excuse me? We don't 'jack up' our prices. Just so you know I think you are..."

A man in a black jacket walked in and Madeline stopped, watching as he walked along their jewelry cases and then he glanced up, saying, "I'm just looking," so she turned back to the older man and started over, in an even tone now. "Just so you know, a 'spectacular' ten or twelve-carat emerald necklace, with the stones unenhanced, meaning no fillers, will cost at least $500,000, or more. But I can find 'stunning' for you, from Cartier or Van Cleef & Arpels, for around two hundred thousand dollars. Or so." Which was more or less true, although she'd never sold a necklace that expensive before.

The man furrowed his brows. "Sounds like highway robbery to me."

Madeline muttered under her breath, "Then you need to have your hearing checked."

He headed to the door, but stopped, and turned back to her, "So would you be able to find an emerald necklace, at least twelve carats, in four days, or not? If yes, I'm interested, definitely interested."

Madeline managed a nod.

The man took a slim gold case out of his jacket pocket, pulled out a business card, and dropped it on the counter. "Call me then when you have a...what did you call it, a 'stunning' emerald necklace? Just make it worth my time." He looked dismissively around the store and walked out.

Madeline glanced at his business card on the counter, then walked over and picked it up. The card was printed on heavy, gray stock and embossed. She ran her fingers across the raised lettering. His business card was expensive, but the man could be just a blowhard; a waste of time. She knew the type.

Still, wouldn't Abby be astonished if she made such a big sale while she was in Chicago? Totally astonished. However, before Madeline spent any time tracking down a $200,000 necklace for the man, she needed to have a sense he had that kind of money. She went on Google and typed in 'Harley A. Atherton,' from his business card, and a page with seven links popped up. Madeline clicked on the first one, and a slick, dark blue and gray website opened, with men carrying assault rifles. She scanned the page; Harley owned a private military contracting company, Atherton Global Security, that provided training and development programs for law enforcement, security professionals, and military personnel in the U.S. as well as overseas. She skimmed the long list of weapons and sniper training classes and tactics. She paused at the next page with the bold headline, "Facility for Special Operations," glancing at the photos of a one-hundred-acre training center in Holyoke that included indoor and outdoor gun ranges, urban reproductions, a driving track, and even an artificial lake. The last page titled, "Elite Forces Experience" included background on their contractors, all of them ex-military, most of them with a Special Operations background that included the Navy Seals, Delta Force, and Marine Raiders. She read the last subhead, "Experts in Close Quarter Combat Available." So, the company provided trained and armed soldiers too.

Harley Atherton was definitely not their typical over-educated, ultra-liberal Boston customer.

* * *

Madeline decided that Harley might be worth the effort, but just to be sure she went on Dunn and Bradstreet's database. After one click, she knew the company was privately held, with Harley listed as the sole owner, who had moved to Massachusetts three years before from Florida. However, no net worth information was available. She did find his home address in Milton, an upscale suburb just ten miles from downtown Boston, and she typed it into a real estate website. Two pages of photos came up. Harley's house, or rather his mansion sat on two acres in the expensive suburb and was valued at eleven million dollars.

Yes, Harley Atherton was definitely worth the effort.

The store was busy for the next three hours, and then in a lull, she went back to her office.

She would show the very rich Harley Atherton what a 'clerk' could do.

* * *

At her desk, Madeline picked up the phone. From her nine years as a gem dealer, she knew all the good ones, so she called Sam, in New York's Diamond District. The man had at least a million dollars of loose stones in his inventory. Even more important, Sam was connected to an exclusive network of top gem dealers in the US, dominated by Israelis and Persians, who sold gemstones to the high-end jewelry brands, as well as estate-level jewelry pieces to upscale retailers. These dealers were all wealthy, almost exclusively male, and continually on the road, traveling to U.S. and international gem shows.

Reputation was everything in the gem dealing business, a centuries-old profession that was based on trust. This network routinely brokered million-dollar deals on behalf of each other's clients sealed with only a handshake or a phone call.

Sam answered his cell phone, his voice warm, with a slight Israeli accent.

"So what's up, Madeline? Just hearing the sound of your voice makes my day."

"Sam, you talk like you're in sales. Oh wait, you are in sales. Anyway, I have a big VIP customer who wants an emerald necklace, at least twelve carats.

AAA grade of course, from one of the big names." A pause and she added, "I can pay a hundred and forty thousand, maximum."

Sam wouldn't care what she sold it for, only what she would pay him. In the gem business, the more expensive the piece the lower the mark-up, and Madeline figured if they charged around $200,000 they could make a profit of approximately $60,000 if a sale—which was a big if—to Harley went through. Which sounded like a lot of money, and was a lot of money, but Coda Gems' expenses now were very high. A problem that was sort of her fault; she'd talked Abby into relocating to their new, high-priced location.

"When do you need it by?" asked Sam.

"I need it in four days. It's an anniversary present so there's no date flexibility. Do you think you can you do it?"

"No promises of course, but it shouldn't be a problem. I'll email you photos of what I find by tomorrow morning. It's important you say?"

"Yes. Very. And thank you, as usual."

"I'm on it," said Sam, and hung up.

Relieved, Madeline hung up the phone. Sam had never let her down.

So far.

Chapter Two

When Madeline walked into her condo building on Boston's Channel Center Street that night the concierge at the desk looked up and nodded towards the sofa in the small lobby. And there was Felix, tall, blonde, and handsome, in blue jeans, a white shirt, and a leather jacket. His standard work attire. He stood up from the sofa and with a wolfish grin walked up.

Felix was her ex-husband, and after their divorce over three years ago, he'd moved to Chicago. Which was good, except he hadn't stayed there. Six months ago he'd come back, working at *The Boston Globe* again, not as a reporter this time, but as head of their online digital platforms. According to him he still loved the newspaper business but was done with reporting the news. "A grind," he'd said. "I just got tired of it."

Felix had been an investigative reporter when they'd been married, one of the best, and had a Pulitzer Prize to prove it. Madeline thought of him as a journalist on steroids, and the big reason she'd divorced him. The problem had been that once he was on the track of a story, everything else became secondary, nothing else mattered, and that included her. He'd leave for days at a time, and it wasn't unusual for her not to know exactly where he was, or when he'd be home. Although even when he was home if his eyes were open, he was usually on his laptop in the study, working.

And now, surprisingly, after he'd moved back to Boston, Felix had told her he wanted to start "seeing" her again, his term. A more exact status still undefined. Madeline's first thought was absolutely never-in-a-million-years-never but she did have to think about it. She had missed him, well

12

she'd missed the good parts. The bad parts still made her furious when she thought about it. But then she had decided that maybe, since he wasn't an investigative reporter anymore, that just possibly it was worth a shot, a very small one. Tiny even.

However, at dinner the week before he told her that he'd just switched back over to the News Unit at *The Globe*. And she froze when he told her, offhandedly, that he was an investigative reporter once again, on their "Spotlight" team, the oldest, continuously operating newspaper investigative unit in the country. The news unit he'd worked in when they'd been married, the biggest bad part of their marriage.

Felix had told, her smiling, "It will be so good to be back on the 'Spotlight' team," adding, "I haven't stopped missing it since I left. I've missed it every day, but of course, I won't be as wrapped up in it as I used to be."

Which led to his long, tedious explanation of why it would be different this time. She'd barely listened.

As they were getting ready to leave the restaurant that night, he'd asked her to come home with him after dinner "for coffee." Madeline knew what that meant, and she told him, "Definitely no. That's just not a good idea."

"Why?"

"A leopard can't change its spots. Now that you're with 'Spotlight' you'll be totally absorbed by whatever investigation you're working on. It won't even matter what it is. So no, I definitely want no part of that, at all."

"Don't worry, it will be fine," and he went on and on yet again about why it was a great idea for them to get back together. She kept glancing at her watch out of the corner of her eye; she just wanted the evening to be over. They finally left the restaurant, and she said goodbye on the sidewalk, "This is goodbye, Felix. A real goodbye. And I do wish you the best. We shouldn't see each other again. I have nothing more to say, I am talked out," and she cut across the busy street to her car, and drove away.

That evening, in the lobby of her condo building, Felix leaned forward as if to give her a kiss, but stopped, saying, "You don't write, you don't call, you..."

Madeline didn't want to talk to Felix in front of the staff, so she said, "Let's go upstairs." She led him to the elevator and punched the button for the 11th floor.

"I hope this isn't inconvenient," he'd said. "But I decided it would be best to connect, in person, since you're not returning my calls. There's something else I want to say."

She looked at him. It had better be good.

Once they were inside her condo she went to the kitchen and poured a glass of white wine for herself and brewed a cup of heavy-jolt coffee for him. The man lived on caffeine.

He began, "At dinner last week, our conversation..." He shrugged, "It was, let's say, unfinished."

"Maybe for you. Not for me." She didn't like to talk about it, since all the old hurts would come creeping back.

She handed Felix his cup of Columbian coffee, black of course. They sat at the kitchen counter and Felix began, running his index finger around the rim of his coffee cup. "I just think there is something still there. Between us I mean. And we should at least explore it. See where it goes."

"We tried that, for three years, remember? I've been there, done that."

Felix shrugged. "There were times it was good. Very good."

"Until it wasn't. Like I told you at dinner, it doesn't work when divorced people get back together. There should be a law against it. It doesn't even work in the movies, well not in the good ones anyway."

"I wasn't suggesting we get married again."

"So you said," and she downed her glass of wine. "But a relationship, of any kind, just won't work, especially since you'll be a reporter on 'Spotlight' again and..."

"Senior Investigative Reporter."

She twirled her empty glass of wine in her fingers. "Look, we got divorced for a reason. A good one. I got tired of always being second."

Felix held up his hand, "No need to go over all that again. Mistakes were made."

"I'm certainly aware of that, but I'm just not interested."

"Well, that was rude. Like I said, we should at least..."

"No."

"It will be different now."

"Really? Where have I heard that before? Felix, I am sorry, but we are truly over. As in 'caput', and let me throw in a 'finito' too."

He stared down at the countertop and then looked up, his blue eyes intense, "I like it when you talk to me in Latin. It's quite sexy."

Madeline had to smile, even though the conversation was frustrating. They talked for another half an hour, until she finally said, "Felix. It's late, and I have nothing more to say except, 'Good night.' We're both just better off not being together. It's for the best, seriously. We shouldn't see each other again because what's the point? We are over."

He got to his feet, slowly, stretching, like a cat. He said, shaking his head. "Fine then. I hear you, but I don't agree. Tell you what though, if you change your mind, just whistle." And then Felix added the famous lines from the Humphrey Bogart and Lauren Bacall movie, *To Have and Have Not*, and he said, "'If you want me just whistle. You know how to whistle don't you? You just put your lips together and blow.'" With a half-smile he turned and walked down the hall to the door, closing it quietly behind him.

The man had a knack for dramatic exits and a memory for classic movie lines. But in the long run, Felix was toxic. Interesting, fascinating, even, but toxic for the soul. She read a book for half an hour, turned off the light, and was asleep two minutes later.

* * *

Madeline woke up early that next morning, thinking of Felix. For about a second. She had things to do. After she showered, she checked her computer before she got dressed just to see if Sam had gotten back to her. He had. Sam, God bless him, had sent her photos of two gleaming emerald necklaces, one by Cartier and the other by Harry Winston, the most exclusive brands in the US. And typical Sam, he'd also attached appraisals for both from the Gemological Institute of America.

The first photo was of a Harry Winston necklace with an eleven-carat emerald surrounded by over four carats of diamonds, and after she reviewed the appraisal, she decided a price of $185,000 was a fair one for Harley. The photo of the Cartier necklace, the more striking of the two, was of a gleaming, fourteen-carat emerald on a heavy platinum chain and her first instinct was to price it at $220,000, but she needed this sale, so she went with $200,000. She sent a text to Sam, thanking him, and then she sent the photos to Harley with descriptions of the necklaces and the price for each.

She wrote in his text, "Harley, let me know if you're interested. I can have them sent here and you can let me know what you think."

Harley would be happy, she thought. He should be since both necklaces were indeed stunning.

* * *

Over her usual breakfast of a bagel with too much cream cheese, Madeline picked up *The Boston Globe*. Under the blaring front-page headline of a hunting death, she read that a Wallace Wright, the CFO at Raytheon, Boston's big air and missile developer had been killed in a deer hunting accident outside of Deerfield in New Hampshire the day before. The article ended with the usual statement that his death was under investigation by the local police, the District Attorney's Office, and the New Hampshire State Police. She skipped the paragraph that tallied the number of accidental hunting deaths in the state over the last twenty years.

Which reminded Madeline that she'd never asked Abby if she'd brought her Sig Sauer pistol with her when they'd moved the store to Newbury Street. Madeline had been uncomfortable when she'd learned six months before that her partner was, as Madeline had put it, 'packing heat.'

"First of all," Abby had said at the time, "nobody talks like that anymore. And secondly, we are vulnerable as you know, since jewelry stores are a prime robbery target in any big city, and that includes Boston. Anyway, I want to be prepared, just in case."

Assuming then that Abby had brought it with her to the new store, where was it? Madeline knew Abby's pistol wasn't in their safe since she was in and out of the safe every day. Besides Abby would never ever keep her gun in the safe.

"Having the gun in my desk makes more sense, it's just easier to get to," Abby had once told her. Abby was from the Midwest, a region of practical women.

Madeline had then suggested that Abby wear her gun strapped around her waist "...in a calf-skin leather holster. Nice and convenient. Black of course, so it will go with everything." Which Abby hadn't found all that funny.

Curious now, Madeline folded up the newspaper and set it aside. The gun, if Abby had brought it to Newbury Street, would be in her desk, so Madeline checked the top drawers. No pistol. And it wasn't in the middle drawers either, filled with neat rows of alphabetized file folders. But the bottom drawer on the right was locked, so that must be where it was. Abby must have locked the drawer before she left for Chicago, but still, she should have given her a key. What if Madeline ever needed Abby's gun? If Coda Gems was going to have a weapon on the premises, she should at least have access to it, even if she didn't exactly know how to shoot.

So maybe it was about time she learned? Yes, it was definitely time she learned how to shoot. She should check into gun ranges and sign up for their gun school. She'd take a lesson or two, and know how to shoot, just like Annie Oakley, her childhood hero. Growing up she'd watched endless re-runs of the TV series with her older sister. Now, years later, Madeline decided it was never too late to learn.

The more she thought about it, the better she liked the idea and went online, and after ten minutes she had booked a lesson at a gun range in Mansfield, south of Boston. The best part was that she could apply for a firearms license immediately after the class, one that included a concealed carry permit after she completed their three-hour Basic Firearms Safety Class. Perfect. All it took was three clicks and her credit card and she was enrolled.

She sighed and looked at the clock. It was almost 12:30 and she thought she'd have heard from Harley by now. It looked like he was nothing but a blowhard after all. Then just before one o'clock, Madeline received a text from him, "I want to see both necklaces. Right away. Let me know when they will arrive."

She said "Hallelujah!" out loud, and called Sam, her gem dealer. "My customer wants to see both necklaces, so can you have them sent to me overnight?"

"No problem."

She sent Harley a text that the necklaces would be at Coda Gems the next day, and he replied he'd be there at three pm. Madeline smiled. It seemed that a big sale to Harley could actually happen.

* * *

Madeline went to what she called her 'gun school' class that evening. There were three geeky twenty-something guys in the class, stereotypical video gamers, except now they had loaded weapons. She avoided eye contact.

Two things surprised her about the class, the first was that the pistol was heavier than it looked, and the second was that it would take sixty days before she could get a gun license, but it would be worth it. She thought having a concealed carry gun license in her wallet, along with her Boston Public Library card and her Massachusetts driver's license would be a nice balance.

* * *

The emerald necklaces arrived the next morning and Madeline studied the appraisals again and examined the pieces under her digital microscope. Both of them were superb; the cut of the stones was flawless, and the stones a deep green, with a triple AAA grading from the Gemological Institute, the highest rating possible.

At precisely 3:00 two men walked into the store, and she recognized one of them as Harley's son. He was again in an expensive suit, this one a dark charcoal gray. But no Harley. The son stood aside as the second man, in his late 30's, also in a suit and tie but who was built like an offensive lineman introduced himself as Edgar Rice, the SVP of Operations at Atherton Global Security, and then he introduced Harley's son, Chase Atherton.

"Harley had to fly unexpectedly to Paris yesterday afternoon, and since he wasn't sure when he'd be back, he asked me to come by and take a look at the necklaces you had sent in," said Edgar.

Chase stepped forward, "Yes, we're here to take a look at his 'anniversary present.'"

She didn't miss the sarcasm in the last part.

"So if you don't mind..." said Chase.

Edgar glanced at him but didn't say anything.

Madeline did mind, but could hardly say so. If Harley couldn't come himself, he should have called her. She led the two men to the office and took the emerald necklaces out of the safe.

The three of them sat at a pale blue granite conference table, and Madeline arranged the jewelry on a black velvet pad in front of them. She talked for several minutes about the cut and carat weight of the emeralds, mentioning the AAA rating three times until Chase interrupted.

"How much are they again?"

She told them the prices.

"So roughly two hundred grand for each?" said Chase.

"Roughly, yes," said Madeline.

He exchanged a look with Edgar and muttered, "Some present."

Edgar took off his glasses, his gray eyes piercing as he picked up a necklace, studying the emeralds, and then he reached for the appraisals. Chase barely glanced at the necklaces, watching Edgar. After five minutes Edgar set the paperwork back on the table with only one comment, "Very thorough appraisals."

The two men looked at each other again, and Madeline broke the silence. "The emeralds in both are..."

Chase interrupted, "Has Olivia seen these necklaces?"

"Olivia?" asked Madeline.

"My father's wife," he snapped.

No love lost there, she thought as she said, "No, she hasn't seen them."

"Who picked out these two necklaces? Was it you?" asked Chase. It sounded like an accusation.

"Yes, but Harley was quite specific about the quality and emerald weight of the necklace he was looking for. I sent him two photos, he liked both and said to have the necklaces sent here overnight. So I did."

She handed Edgar extra copies of the appraisals, "These are for Harley," she said, and Chase stood up, and then Edgar. Apparently, the meeting was over. A fast meeting thought Madeline, too fast.

She turned to Edgar, "When will Harley be back from Paris?"

"I'm not sure yet. I'll let him know we were here to see you, and the jewelry."

She heard Chase whisper to Edgar, "Besides a necklace, I bet Olivia talks Dad into taking her to Paris for a couple of weeks. She'd live there if she could for God's sake."

At the front door, Madeline thanked them for coming and watched them walk down the street. Chase was a jerk and Edgar a hard-eyed jock. Not exactly a pleasant duo.

Madeline had to do something, and she had to do it now because she suspected Edgar was sure to let Harley know right away, his not-so-good opinion. And the son certainly wouldn't be helpful. Why was he even there in the first place?

She pulled out her cell phone, took five photos of each necklace, and texted them to Harley, with a message, "Edgar and Chase were just here, but I strongly suggest you come and see them for yourself. They are both on the high end of 'stunning'. I can guarantee it will not be a waste of your time."

A minute later Harley sent a text, "I'm flying back from Paris tonight, so I'll be there at three tomorrow with my wife. You better be right."

* * *

That night, at Boston's Logan airport, Chase pulled his black Volvo in front of the British Airways 'Arrivals' sign. Harley stepped off the curb, dropped his leather duffle bag in the back, and slid into the passenger seat.

Harley took out his cell phone and scrolled through his emails, not looking up, as he said, "Why did you go with Edgar to look at the necklaces for Olivia? I certainly don't need your opinion on..."

Chase cut in, "I got a haircut at the Pini Swissa Salon on Newbury Street, which is just above the jewelry store. I ran into Edgar in the lobby."

Harley grunted in reply, then said, "And you both thought they were over-priced." A statement rather than a question.

"Like I told you, I thought they were just average, nice but average, and yes, definitely over-priced," said Chase. "By the way, I didn't care for the blonde woman there. She's a know-it-all type. You should go someplace else."

In the heavy silence, Chase merged his car into the line of airport traffic, and not looking at his father said, "How is Olivia?"

"She's fine. Just fine," said Harley, staring out the window.

"That's good." Chase didn't mean it.

Harley shifted in his seat, "I'm working from home on Thursday. Can you come out to the house in the afternoon around 2:30? I want to go over the materials for stripping down an M4 carbine for next week's training session with the FBI teams."

"Fine, I'll move a couple of meetings around."

"Not that your fancy-ass MBA from M.I.T. will be of much use," added Harley.

Chase's hands gripped the steering wheel, hard, and he gunned his car around a lumbering MBTA bus in front of him. "And how was Paris? Why was it so last minute? You never said why you had to go."

"I obviously thought it was important or I wouldn't have gone. Turns out it wasn't. Nothing the guy dug up for me was any use. What he had proved nothing, and was a waste of my time. I told him not to call me again unless he had solid evidence."

"Evidence of what?"

"Never mind," and Harley yawned, staring out the window, the night pierced by flashes of approaching traffic. "Wallace's funeral is tomorrow, right? I never knew he was a deer hunter."

"Yes, it's at eleven o'clock."

"Anything new?"

"I read that the cops think there's a possibility the shooting wasn't a hunting accident, which means it could become a murder investigation."

Harley jarred forward in his seat, staring at his son. "What? Murder?"

"Yes, murder. The approximate spot where the shooter was standing has been established, but the cops didn't find any shell casings, and the ground was covered by leaves, so no footprints. There wasn't any evidence at all, except for the bullet, and they've run ballistics on that. Supposedly it was a straight shot to the heart, which doesn't seem like it was all that accidental. The cops thought the spot looked cleaned up too, so I'm sure that's why they are considering it as a possible homicide." Chase's eyes flickered between his side and rearview mirrors. "You know how cops are, they are born suspicious. And, given that he was the CFO at Raytheon and they do a lot of government work here and internationally, and...well, that's probably another reason the cops might be thinking it wasn't an accident. In my opinion."

Harley sighed. "You don't know what you're talking about. Wallace was just a finance guy, and he was shot, accidentally, by another hunter. I'm sure it was an accident. Probably by some kid who got scared, covered up his tracks, and left the scene."

"Could be, but more people die in deer hunting accidents by falling out of tree stands than getting shot by other hunters."

"How do you know that?"

"Because I can read. It wouldn't surprise me if they'd want to take a look at Wallace's current and old business dealings in the U.S. You know they might want to talk to you."

"Me? Christ!"

"Well, it's not every day the CFO of a big company like Raytheon gets killed by a high-powered rifle. At least the newspapers said that's what it was. After all, Wallace did work for you."

"That? It was a long time ago, years ago. I can't be bothered. You can take care of that if it comes up."

"Fine, but are you going to his funeral? The New Hampshire State Police might be there since his death is still under investigation."

"No, I'm not going, I don't have time," said Harley. "Besides, I've hardly talked to Wallace in the last eighteen years or so, not since Algeria. Christ, what a mess that was. Anyway, I'm busy tomorrow."

Harley went back to the emails on his phone until Chase took the Milton exit and drove down a dark side road and then a right onto a long, winding drive. He stopped in front of a three-story brick mansion dramatically bathed by soft landscape lighting. Harley mumbled, "Thanks." He clambered out of the car and grabbed his bag. "Next time don't pick me up in a shitty coupe. I pay you enough so get a decent car for Christ's sake."

* * *

Thirty minutes later Chase pulled into the long, dark driveway of his home in Concord, a little more than twenty miles from downtown Boston, but another world away. His house in the upscale suburb was isolated, with no neighbors for at least half a mile. The Prairie-Style house, with its flat roof, overhanging eaves, and windows in horizontal groups blended in with the forest of pines. Walden Pond was only half a mile away.

Once inside, he walked down the hall to his study, a room his father called 'A Victorian Nightmare.' The heavy wingback chairs and sofa were upholstered in plum-colored damask, a mahogany, claw-footed desk stood on a Persian rug by the fireplace, and the drapes on the study's fifteen-foot-tall windows were a deep, dark red. The only thing missing was Sherlock Holmes with an English briar pipe. Chase didn't smoke a pipe, but he did smoke cigars, the hand-rolled Cuban kind.

He went to the wide fireplace, opened the flu, and after he had a fire going, he went to the kitchen and poured three fingers of Glenlivet in a glass. Back in his study, Chase set his drink on an ebony end table and shoved the bottom log with a poker until sparks flew. Only then did he sit down, and carefully cut off the tip of his cigar. He lit it, a trail of smoke drifting up to the high ceiling.

He picked up his drink and stared around his study. So, Harley was giving Olivia a $200,000 emerald necklace. He stared at the claw-footed desk that had been his mother's. He could almost see her sitting at the desk, her blonde head bent over her worn copy of *Wildflowers of New England Field Guide*, her reading glasses delicately poised on the end of her nose. Even though it had been nearly two years now he sometimes had a hard time believing she was dead.

He lifted his drink and said in a whisper, "Here's a toast to you, Mom," and drained his glass. "Dad could have given you a two-hundred-thousand-dollar necklace but he never did, did he? He could have at least done that."

Chapter Three

Harley was always at the office by 7:00 am every day, and the next morning was no exception.

He got off at the executive floor of Atherton Global's corporate offices at 60 State Street a commanding office tower in Boston's financial district, and headed down the hall to his huge office, not bothering to glance in the small one next to his. Penelope, his assistant for over thirty-five years, would already be at her desk, and as Harley pulled out his leather desk chair, she walked in.

"Good morning, Harley. Welcome back." In her late-fifties and leaning to stout, she wore a beige silk blouse, brown skirt, and brown oxfords. Even her short hair was brown. She looked unremarkable, as usual.

Her memory was anything but.

Penelope remembered every client Atherton Global had had over the last thirty-five years, along with important details of their legal agreement, which usually ran over a hundred pages, mostly for SWAT training, guerilla tactics, weapons drills, and marksmanship training. Then there were the contracts with foreign governments that were almost as long, although those were primarily for Atherton Global mercenaries, where they made their real money. Although times had changed, and mercenaries was a term rarely used anymore by Atherton Global or their clients. These days they were called 'private military contractors.' Whatever they were called, they still did the same thing. These contractors had become a necessity for the down-sized U.S. armed forces. In Iraq and Afghanistan, one in four U.S. personnel had been an armed private contractor.

Harley grunted a "Good Morning," and opened his computer. "I need you to go to Wallace's funeral this morning. Someone from the 'Old Days' should be there, and Lucy will appreciate it. His funeral is at 11:00."

"I know, I was already planning to go. It's at the cathedral, so I'll leave at 10:30. I thought I'd stay a little after, too, and catch up with Lucy. Wallace and I stayed in touch you know, and I…"

Harley interrupted, "It's good you're going. Tell Lucy I was flying back from Paris for his service, but my plane was delayed."

Penelope nodded. "I sent flowers from you to the house yesterday."

"You did? Excellent."

"Anything special you want me to say to Lucy? It's been a long time."

"No. Just that I asked you to go on my behalf."

Penelope hesitated at the door. "It's too bad Wallace died the way he did."

"Why did you say that?" He looked up, startled, "What do you mean?"

"I mean getting shot by another hunter. You know they still haven't found out who fired the rifle that killed him."

"Oh. There's a chance they'll turn themselves in, but only after they get lawyered up. By the way, the New Hampshire State Police might be at the funeral. If they ask you about Wallace, just say you barely remember him."

"No problem. What a tragedy though."

"Yes, it is a tragedy," said Harley, flipping through the stack of papers in his in-box.

Penelope went back to her desk and went over Harley's schedule for the day. She saw that he'd added in a meeting at a store called Coda Gems. She looked up their address, 18 Newbury Street, and included that in his calendar. She'd have to ask him about the appointment when she took in his mail in a couple of minutes.

Even though it had been years since Wallace had worked for Harley, Penelope remembered him very well. He had been just like her, everyone he ever met or knew who was connected to their business was permanently stored in his memory. Back then he'd once told her they were like a couple of elephants. "Asian, not African," he said, tugging at his earlobe, "they have smaller ears."

Harley should have sent his son Chase to Wallace's funeral since he wasn't going, but she wasn't all that surprised. There'd been an undercurrent of tension between father and son for the last two years, ever since Harley divorced Chase's mother. But Harley never talked about that, or about what had happened in the middle of the divorce, which was fine with her.

One thing was for sure, she did not care for Olivia, the new wife. Maybe, Penelope thought, she'd come to like her over time. After a couple of seconds, she decided probably not. There was something about Olivia that she couldn't quite put her finger on.

* * *

Since Harley and his wife were both coming into the store at three that afternoon, Madeline put on a suit that morning, one of only two she owned, this one black and Italian, with a peplum jacket and straight skirt. She slipped on a pair of high heels and glanced in her full-length mirror. She looked like the defense attorney in a high-profile, white-collar criminal trial. Adding a Hermes scarf wouldn't help.

She clasped a necklace of delicate, eighteen-karat gold links around her neck, and looked in the mirror again. Better, sort of. She left for the store.

* * *

Just before two o'clock, Madeline noticed an older woman in a sable hat, with a brown coat over a brown skirt staring at their jewelry display in the window. And then the woman walked in.

"I'd like to see the Patek watch in the window please," she said, glancing around the store.

"Of course." Madeline took it out and displayed it on a black pad on the counter in front of her. "This particular Patek..."

"Trust me, I know all about Patek watches," the woman said with a smile. "Too much sometimes, I think. My boss collects them." She glanced at the price tag. "Seven thousand five hundred is a good price for this watch."

27

"It is."

The woman picked up the watch and strapped the silver band around her wrist. "It's a man's watch but I don't care." She turned her wrist, admiring the watch. "I believe every woman needs a reliable timepiece." She looked up, "Even a low-end Patek is better than any other watch, at any price."

Which Madeline thought was interesting. Harley had said exactly the same thing when he'd looked at it three days before.

The woman said, "My boss told me this morning that you had a Patek, at a fair price, relatively speaking that is. And this one is waterproof, right?"

Madeline nodded.

"Perfect, because I am a kayaker. I'm out on the water a couple of times a week, rain or shine. I guess you could call it an obsession. Well anyway, that's what my boss calls it." Penelope beamed, "I'll take it." She took off the watch and handed it to Madeline.

In the five months since they'd moved to Newbury Street, not one customer had asked to see the watch in the window. Except for Harley. So, the woman must work for him, but Madeline didn't say anything. One of the first things Madeline had learned about the very rich was that you never talked about them to other people; they didn't like it.

"I've wanted to buy a Patek for years," the woman said. "My name is Penelope by the way," and she handed Madeline a credit card. She walked around the store, peering in their glass cases, looking up every now and then as Madeline rang up the sale and set the watch in one of Coda Gems' matte-black boxes, their name embossed in gold on the lid. Penelope walked up then, signed the receipt, and Madeline slid the box in a black bag and handed it to her.

"You have a lovely store," said Penelope. "Thank you again. I'm taking the rest of the day off since this is a sad day." She looked at Madeline, "It's a long story," and she sailed out the door.

Maybe Penelope would show the watch to Harley. Or not. It didn't really matter. She was a nice customer.

* * *

At 2:55, Harley walked into Coda Gems, followed by a tall, striking-looking woman with a hawk nose and long brown hair pulled back, her gleaming hair clip dotted with emerald stones, probably real. She was dressed in a dark green silk suit and was in her mid-forties Madeline guessed. The woman wore no other jewelry except for a big diamond on her left hand, which had to be at least five carats.

Harley introduced the woman as his wife, Olivia, and the two women nodded. Madeline walked the couple into the office, and they sat at the blue conference table. She asked if they'd like coffee, tea, or water, and both said no.

Madeline arranged the Cartier necklace with the 14-carat emerald in front of them, and Harley picked it up, examining it under the light of the table lamp. This time she went into detail about the carat weight of the emeralds, and the marquis-cut of the stone. She explained, "The most important criteria in evaluating emeralds however is the color. As you can see, this one is a lush green with very high brilliance."

Olivia listened closely, but Harley kept glancing at his watch.

Madeline continued, "First of all, the emeralds in both necklaces are natural, not lab created. However, bear in mind that 95% of all natural emeralds have slight surface fissures. Like the emerald in that one," and she nodded to the Cartier necklace, "which has been enhanced with resin fillings so the fissures are virtually undetectable. By the way, that condition is pointed out in the appraisal."

Harley lay the necklace back on the velvet pad. "And the other one?"

Madeline brought out the Harry Winston necklace with emeralds and diamonds and displayed it on another black velvet pad in front of Harley.

He stared at it, "Both of them looked better in the photos you sent, much better. I thought you said they were stunning. Well, they're not."

Olivia ignored Harley and picked up the Cartier necklace, saying to Harley, "This necklace is quite striking, the emerald is such a beautiful green. It's breathtaking really. I love it." The woman had an accent, slight, but definitely an accent; French thought Madeline.

Harley ignored her and said to Madeline. "Send both of them back. I'm not interested in either one, and they are over-priced. Edgar thought so too."

Olivia didn't pay any attention to him as she reached for the back-lit vanity mirror on the conference table and clasped the necklace around her neck. She stared at her reflection and turned to Harley. "Yes, this is exactly what I want." She paused, "But Harley, why on earth is Edgar involved in my anniversary present?"

"Because he is in charge of all of our purchasing. And I trust him."

"Well, he should stick to the price of AK-47's for God's sake, or paper clips. I don't know why you put up with him, basically, he's just a thug."

"You said the necklaces were stunning," he said, ignoring her and turning to Madeline. "They aren't, they're just average." He grunted to Olivia, "Let's go. I don't have time for this. Neither one is good enough."

Olivia said to Madeline, "My mother had an emerald necklace like this once. A long time ago, in another life. I remember…" And then she stopped. In the silence she took off the emerald necklace, and held it in her hand, staring at the deep green stone. "Yes, this is perfect," she repeated, and said to Harley, "And it's not overpriced."

"You don't know what you're talking about."

"But I do know. I know all about emeralds, and this necklace is extraordinary. This is the one I want."

Harley stared at her. "But I can find…"

"There is no need."

He sighed and said to Madeline, nodding to the necklace in his wife's hand, "So you are asking $200,000 for this, even though the emerald has cracks?"

"Not cracks, just several slight fissures, which are natural, and have been corrected by resin. And I am offering you a good price for the necklace. If you want an unenhanced emerald, and they are quite rare by the way, the cost of this piece would be over five hundred thousand."

"Send both of them back," repeated Harley.

Olivia leaned towards Harley and their eyes locked. "Harley, don't be difficult about this." She put the emerald necklace around her neck again, staring at her reflection. "I love it."

Harley drummed his fingers on the table, "I told you I—"

"Harley, this necklace will be a wonderful anniversary present. Really wonderful. You are a generous husband."

Harley's cell phone rang and he pulled it out of his pocket, looking at the caller ID. He said into the phone, "Did you get the info? I told you I wanted actual proof. What did you find out?" A pause as he stared at Olivia, who had taken off the necklace, running the platinum chain through her fingers. He turned and walked over to the railing, still talking on his phone.

"The emeralds in my mother's necklace were enhanced too, with oil," Olivia said to Madeline. "Most emeralds are. I remember because she told me that one night. The night there was a—"

Harley raised his voice as he said forcefully into the phone, "I told you I need verification immediately. Let me know as soon as you have it. You should have had it over three weeks ago." Harley held the phone closer to his ear, Olivia, toying with the necklace, wasn't looking at Harley but Madeline could tell she was paying close attention to his side of the conversation. Then Harley shouted into the phone, "Well, see that you do! How hard can it be?"

He clicked off his phone, and then it rang again. He barked into it, "What now?" and walked down towards the door listening, then said, "Well, call Chase, and tell him I said he's got to take the basic firearms class again." A pause, then, "I don't care what he thinks. You tell my son I want his ass at the Center by 11:00 tomorrow morning for another Small Arms session. Tell him I said if he doesn't improve his score, I'll fire his sorry ass."

Harley listened for another minute and looked back at Olivia, "I have to go to the office. I'll see you later," and he stormed out.

* * *

After Harley left, Olivia handed the necklace to Madeline. "I'll talk him into it tonight. He just needs a little convincing. Don't send it back."

"Fine. I'll hold onto both of them for two days."

"Good. Do you have any other emerald jewelry?"

Madeline set both necklaces in a drawer and led Olivia to a section of a glass case for their emerald pieces, glittering necklaces, earrings, bracelets, and rings. Olivia scanned the jewelry, "None of them are exactly exceptional, are they?" She walked to the glass case of diamonds, saying over her shoulder, "I would like a cup of tea, chamomile would be good. And I take cream, not milk."

Madeline walked over to their Keurig in an alcove, dropped in a pod of chamomile, and hit brew. At least they had half-and-half in the fridge, which would just have to do.

Olivia said, not looking up, "I need to see the Cartier necklace again."

"No problem," said Madeline. She took out the necklace and set it in front of Olivia. At least the woman knew what she wanted. The only good thing about her.

Olivia sat down on a stool, pulled the vanity mirror closer, and clasped the necklace around her neck again. Olivia leaned forward, staring at her reflection when her cell phone rang and she pulled it out of her jacket pocket. She listened for a moment and said, "Yes, I'm still here." A silence, and then, "Fine. I'm leaving now. I'll see you at home." She set her phone on the counter while she unhooked the necklace and handed it to Madeline. "Never mind about the tea. I'll be in touch tomorrow morning."

Olivia stood and walked out the door.

Madeline watched her leave; even her walk was commanding, arrogant. She sighed and thought that yes, maybe Abby was right, maybe she was just too sensitive. Maybe she did need to lighten up. Madeline put the necklace back in their safe and walked back to the front of the store. Only then did she notice Olivia's cell phone on the counter.

* * *

She grabbed Olivia's cell phone and ran out the door and saw her striding down the sidewalk half a block away. Madeline called out to her, but Newbury Street was jammed with the usual snarled and honking traffic and Olivia didn't hear. Madeline threw the lock on the store's front door and hurried after her. She watched as Olivia stepped off the curb, jaywalking across the busy street as the light changed, and Madeline shouted again, running now in between the cars as she zig-zagged down the street until she was right behind Olivia.

Just then a dusty, brown car careened around the corner of Dartmouth Street onto Newbury Street, the tires squealing as Madeline called out Olivia's name again. Madeline glanced behind her and saw the car, now less than five feet away, bearing down on her when she suddenly felt two hands on her back, and with a mighty heave Madeline was shoved out of the way of the car and she fell to the pavement. Out of the corner of her eye, she saw Olivia, who must have pushed her, almost lose her balance, and then catch herself at the last second.

The car missed Olivia and Madeline by inches, close enough to Madeline's head she was staring at the tread of the black tires as she lay on the street, stunned by her fall. She heard the brown car barely slow as it careened around the corner.

And then Olivia was standing over Madeline's motionless body, protecting her from the rush-hour traffic that now swirled dangerously close around the two women. There was the sound of brakes as oncoming traffic stopped, and doors slammed as several cars pulled over and the drivers jumped out.

Olivia bent over Madeline and shouted, "Are you alright?"

Madeline nodded her head, unable to speak, the wind knocked out of her.

"You're sure?" said Olivia.

This time Madeline managed a "Yes" as two men and a woman ran up to help. Madelinewaved them away, reached for Olivia's hand, and pulled herself to her feet.

"I had to get you out of the way," explained Olivia. "There was a car that—"

"I know. I didn't see it until the last second." She took a long breath. "Thanks."

Olivia took Madeline's arm and the two women stepped onto the sidewalk. Madeline walked gingerly and said to Olivia, "Well, nothing seems to be broken."

"People in the U.S. don't know how to drive," said Olivia, "and Boston drivers are the worst. Almost as bad as Algiers—" and she stopped. Then she said, "I'll go with you back to the store. You're sure you're alright?"

Madeline nodded.

"Did you see the driver?" asked Olivia five minutes later. Madeline unlocked the store's front door and they walked inside.

"No, I didn't see the driver," Madeline said with a grim smile. "You knocked me to the ground, remember?"

Once inside, Olivia turned to Madeline, looking her over. "Did you hit your head on the pavement?"

"I don't think so. I don't remember, actually." Madeline put the palm of her hand on her highlighted blonde hair and looked at it. No blood, which was good.

"Do you have a flashlight?" asked Olivia.

Madeline opened a drawer by the cash register and handed Olivia a flashlight.

"Stand still for just a minute," and she shone the flashlight in both Madeline's eyes, then clicked it off.

"What are you doing?" asked Madeline.

"Just checking. You're fine."

"Are you a doctor or something?"

"No." When Madeline looked at her, Olivia added, "Girl Scouts."

Madeline brushed the dirt off her jacket and fingered a jagged tear on the right sleeve. She loved the jacket, so she'd have it mended of course. Then she flashed back to those seconds she was lying on the pavement, the black tires of the brown car just inches from her head. No, she wouldn't have it mended, she'd throw it away.

"That was really, really close, wasn't it?" said Madeline. "Thank you again." She pulled Olivia's cell phone out of her pocket and handed it to her. "By the way, here's your cell phone. You left it on the counter. "

"I did?" Olivia suddenly grimaced and turned away, massaging the back of her neck with her right hand.

"Are you alright?" asked Madeline.

"Yes, I'm fine, it's just an old...injury acting up. I was in a bad accident a long time ago."

"I'm sorry to hear that. Would you like that cup of tea now?" said Madeline.

34

She noticed that Olivia's eyes had narrowed in pain.

Olivia shook her head, "No, I should get back. Don't say anything though, not a single word to Harley about the brown car. I saw the driver, it was just a young kid driving too fast and he lost control. Harley sees conspiracies everywhere, and it will only upset him, and I don't want that, especially not now. Anyway, I'll call you tomorrow morning about the necklace." She turned at the door, "You should go see a doctor if you feel dizzy or disoriented in the next twenty-four hours. You'll also likely have some bruises," and she left.

Madeline watched her walk quickly down the street to a black BMW illegally parked. Madeline shivered, she could have been seriously hurt, or worse. Olivia was definitely an entitled woman, and also one, with fast reflexes. She was courageous too.

But Girl Scouts?

* * *

Later that afternoon, cool eyes scanned the weapons in the gun room again. It was too soon, way too soon, but one had to be ready. Not a rifle this time, it needed to be a handgun. Something small. Minutes later a gloved hand reached down to a bottom shelf and grabbed a semi-automatic pistol. Powerful yet compact. Perfect.

Yes, it would be good to have a gun, since it seemed things were going downhill. Fast.

Chapter Four

Madeline woke up that next morning feeling like she hadn't slept at all because she hadn't. She ached all over, and the image of Olivia standing over her, so straight and tall, shielding her from oncoming traffic as she lay dazed on the street was now burned into her memory.

Madeline groaned when she got out of bed but then did fifteen minutes of stretches, which helped a bit. She checked her right forearm. The bruise that hadn't looked all that bad the night before was now a deep, ugly blue, and tender, plus her left knee ached. She cautiously showered and headed to the store. She hoped Olivia had talked Harley into buying the necklace last night. Today could be a great day, or not.

Five minutes after she walked into the store, her cell phone rang.

"I spoke to Harley last night," began Olivia, "and he's agreed to buy the Cartier necklace. The one with the big emerald and platinum chain. For two hundred thousand dollars."

"That is great news, really great news!" Madeline's heart skipped a beat. "Thank you, Olivia, and thank you again for what you did yesterday. You were amazing. You saved my life."

"Well, we women do have to stick together, don't we? Otherwise, nothing will turn out the way we want it to. Nothing. Like I said, though, not a word about that. Not a single word. I told you Harley sees conspiracies everywhere, so I have to be very careful, about everything. Very careful. Especially today. I have to go now, but call Harley's assistant, Penelope about setting up a wire transfer to your bank," and Olivia rattled off a cell number.

"Harley wants it done right away since our anniversary is actually today. Talk about leaving things for the last minute."

"I'll call Penelope now."

"Good," Olivia paused. "As soon as the wire transfer hits your account, bring the necklace out to the house in Milton." She gave Madeline the address. "Three o'clock would be a perfect time. And can you wrap it up, all nice and fancy, with a big pink bow? Harley likes pink, he thinks it's a soothing color," said Olivia with a throaty laugh. "And Madeline, again, not a word about yesterday. Ever." and she hung up. The woman defined abrupt.

Madeline's knee started to ache again, but she ignored it. She called Penelope, who said, "Yes, Olivia said you'd be in touch. And by the way, I am so glad I bought your watch. I can't stop looking at it. I just love it."

Five minutes later the wire transfer was set up, and as Madeline hung up she said, out loud, even though she was alone, "So far so good." She missed Abby; the store was lonely without her, but she didn't want to call her yet with the good news. She'd call Abby after she delivered the necklace. Then she'd let her know that she'd just sold an emerald necklace for $200,000.

Abby would be...astounded.

* * *

The store was quiet the rest of the morning, just a trickle of customers and only seven sales, although one of them was for over $10,000, which made it not a great day, but a pretty good one. They had to be patient since they had a limited advertising budget and were barely a blip on the radar of Boston's affluent.

Madeline was about to close the store and run out to pick up wrapping paper and a bow for Olivia's necklace when the bells on the front door jangled. She looked up as a smiling Abby, in navy slacks and sweater walked in with her suitcase.

Madeline hugged her. "Oh my God, you're back! I can't believe it. I am so glad you're back! But so soon? I thought you were staying in Chicago for another couple of days, maybe even, God forbid, a week. How is your mother?"

"You didn't get my text? I sent it early this morning. Mom is doing well, and Dad arranged to have a nurse come in every day, so there was nothing for me to do except 'hover'. I told Mom I'd come back over Thanksgiving for a week. Besides, I was anxious to get back to the store, you know, see how things are going, and see if you were having any…"

"I told you I'd be just fine."

"Anyway, I was able to get a flight out this morning, so I booked it," said Abby. A pause as she glanced around. "It's too bad you told Martin that he didn't need to come in at all while I was gone. He would have come in. He would have been happy to."

Madeline shrugged. "It was just easier without him here. I told you he makes me crazy."

"Still, you should have had…"

"Abby, like I said, there wasn't any need."

Abby hung up her coat in the closet, set her suitcase in the back, then turned and smiled at her. "I guess I worry too much sometimes."

"That's true," said Madeline, "you do."

"Did anything else happen while I was gone, like an armed robbery or something?"

"I know where your gun is," said Madeline, and Abby's eyes went to the bottom right drawer of her desk. So, Madeline had been right, that's where it was. She said to Abby, "Don't worry, I didn't touch it. I couldn't because you locked the drawer before you left. Anyway, you'll be glad to know I took a gun safety class in Mansfield while you were gone, and I am in the process of getting a gun license, the concealed carry kind. In about seven or eight weeks I'll be a legal gun-slinger with a weapon somewhere on my person."

"You shouldn't take my gun out, ever," warned Abby. "The safety is on, but it is loaded."

"Don't worry, I won't touch your precious gun. Besides, I'll be getting one of my own. Seriously, I am getting a gun."

Abby laughed ironically, "Oh good. That will solve my security concerns," and quickly added, "That was a joke. Really, Madeline, we don't need another gun in the store."

"Oh come on, Abby. I quite like the idea of Coda Gems bristling with weapons."

"Well, I don't. Besides, you could end up accidentally shooting yourself or something."

"We'll talk about that later," said Madeline, who didn't want to have an argument with Abby on her first day back. Still, when she finally had a concealed carry license, and a gun, she intended to take her weapon with her pretty much everywhere. Did people who were armed actually walk differently than other people? She thought they probably did.

Madeline changed the subject. "But, Abby, I do have good news. Great news, actually, but I wanted to wait until the money was in the bank before I said anything. And it will be in an hour or so when the bank wire hits our account." She paused, for dramatic effect.

"Anyway, Abby you're not going to believe this, but I sold an emerald necklace from Sam in New York for two hundred thousand dollars, which will leave us with a net of sixty thousand dollars."

Abby's eyes opened wide. "You did? You're kidding. No, you wouldn't kid about something like that. You really did? I can't believe it! That is wonderful, Madeline."

"It is, isn't it?"

"Although that's sixty thousand dollars before taxes."

A typical Abby comment. Still, Madeline was thrilled she was back.

"Who is paying two hundred grand for a necklace?" said Abby as she walked up to Madeline and high-fived her.

"His name is Harley A. Atherton. The 'A' must stand for 'awesome.' Unfortunately, I don't know what his net worth is, but his home in Milton is worth eleven million dollars."

"Harley Atherton? Never heard of him. But a guy like that is buying an emerald necklace from us? What happened, he just walked in the door out of the blue?"

"He stopped in to look at the Patek in the window," and Madeline gave Abby a condensed and somewhat modified version of his visits. Not mentioning that the first time he came in, Harley had almost walked out twice in a bit of a huff. She ended, "So that's the man, in a nutshell. By the way, he's also a demanding bully."

"Well, it's still amazing. You have a natural gift for sales."

"Trust me, I do not. The man is a total—"

Madeline's cell pinged with a text, and she looked down at her phone, "That's the bank. Harley's wire transfer just came through, so it's official. I have to run out now and buy pink wrapping paper, and the most elegant, pink bow I can find, and deliver the necklace to him by 3:00 this afternoon."

"Pink?"

"Harley likes pink, at least that's what his wife said. But that doesn't mean he is 'evolved'. He's not, not in the least. His wife, by the way, is French, and she's...well I guess she's alright. She does know what she wants."

"You see, Madeline, not all rich people are offensive."

Madeline shrugged. "Maybe so, but maybe not. In my experience, if you let the rich push you around they will take advantage of you."

"How did you get so cynical?"

"Practice," said Madeline over her shoulder as she opened the safe and took out the emerald necklace. "Here, take a look at this," and she handed it to Abby, the heavy emerald pendant hanging between her fingers, "Harley's anniversary present for his wife. What do you think?"

"Good heavens, this necklace is gorgeous," said Abby, spreading the necklace out on the conference table. "And Sam found this for you?"

Madeline nodded, and Abby said, "Well, it is stunning!"

"I know. I told Harley I'd find him a stunning necklace, and so I did."

The two women walked back to the front counter, and Abby said, "You're limping. Why are you limping?"

Madeline didn't want to mention almost getting run down by a car yesterday practically in front of the store. That kind of drama would spoil the moment.

"Oh, it's nothing. I wore a suit yesterday, and high heels if you can believe it. And I tripped, or something. I should throw the high heels away."

"Don't," said Abby. "High heels are good." She sat at her desk and pulled out her computer.

Madeline grabbed her wallet. "I better go, I have to stop home too, and change. If I had pink cowboy boots I'd wear them to Harley's."

"Well, it's a blessing that you don't."

"I'll be back in less than an hour, and then I'll head out to Milton with the necklace. Oh, Abby, I'm so glad you're back. This is turning out to be a perfect day. Let's go out for dinner tonight and celebrate!"

"Yes, this does call for a celebration."

"It does indeed," and she went out the door.

* * *

Madeline was back in the store an hour later with a small shopping bag. She was in her usual black jeans, but now she wore a black Burberry jacket and glossy black cowboy boots. Her idea of dressing up.

She pulled pink wrapping paper and a small, elaborate pink bow out of the bag and grabbed scissors and scotch tape from a drawer. Madeline carefully wrapped Olivia's present in the pink paper and added the bow.

Abby said, "I think it's quite pretty. If you like pink, which I actually do."

"Personally, I think black is good since it goes with everything. I believe it's hard to go wrong with a good, deep black," said Madeline. "However, pink is now, officially, my second favorite color in the universe."

* * *

Twenty minutes later Madeline was heading to Milton on I-93, and forty minutes after that she was in the upscale village. On the passenger seat beside her was the pink-wrapped box with the emerald necklace, and a dozen pink roses she'd picked up at the last minute for Harley. She drove down the leafy, quiet side-road, until her GPS announced in its somber tone, 'You have arrived at your destination.'

Madeline drove through a ten-foot high wrought-iron gate, then past an endless lawn, now a dull, autumn brown, surrounded by hemlock trees. She finally pulled up in front of a brick mansion, with a row of Grecian pillars lining the front, and bars on the windows that masqueraded as slender iron scrolling. If the intent was elegance, it failed, the place looked like a fortress.

A four-car garage stood to the left of the main house, and two smaller brick buildings, with wide windows were set back from the mansion, a car parked in front. Guest houses she thought. To the right of the house was a barn, and several bay horses eyed her curiously from a paddock. She parked on the graveled drive and walked up to the front door of the mansion, the box with the necklace in her hand. She looked around and saw a doorbell set between the iron paws of a rampant lion statue. The place was like a movie set.

Olivia answered the door in ivory slacks and an ivory sweater.

"Your timing is perfect," she said, and led Madeline down a long, wide hallway to a living room with a huge fireplace, and two upholstered sofas in a pale beige, with a third sofa and a matching arm chair in a soft pink leather. Harley really did like pink. Floor-to-ceiling windows on three sides looked out on a wide patio with slate gray tiles and a teak table and chairs under a stand of trees, with more stretches of lawn on either side. She walked up closer to the window. A sloping brick path led down to a wide river below, which must be the Neponset. She heard a door slam somewhere in the house, and distant voices.

Olivia called out, "Harley, your lovely present has arrived."

Harley walked in a minute later, his cell phone in his hand, "Edgar just got here, and Chase is coming any minute. He better not be late. Anyway, I'm expecting a very important call," he said, and reached for the box in Madeline's hand.

He opened it, glanced at the necklace, scrawled his signature on the receipt that Madeline handed him, and turned to Olivia, "Happy Anniversary," he said, and with a quick kiss on the cheek he gave her the box.

His cell phone rang, and he turned away, saying into the phone, "It's about time. What do you have?" and he went across the living room to a side door. Madeline watched him open the door and walk out onto the patio. He stood on gray tiles talking on the phone, and ran his hand through his salt and pepper hair. Then he walked out of view.

42

Olivia watched him, a flicker of worry on her face. "I swear Harley was born with a cell phone attached to his ear. He is not the romantic type. At all." She slid open the Coda Gems box and picked up the gleaming emerald necklace. "Yes, I absolutely, positively love it!" and with a slow smile she laid it out on the table. "It is really beautiful." She looked at Madeline, nodding to the loupe around her neck. "That looks odd, peculiar even. Do you always wear that thing around your neck, like a necklace?"

Madeline fingered the loupe. "I do, I guess. I use it all the time so I don't even think about it." She lifted the loupe to her face, explaining, "It's called a loupe. Just use your thumb and rest it against your cheek like this, and then bring whatever you're examining up close, like this," and she picked up the necklace and focused on the emerald pendant. "It is a beautiful stone, and it's fascinating to examine it this closely. Do you want to take a look?"

Olivia said, "No. I'm sure that's all very interesting. To you."

Madeline handed the necklace back to Olivia, who went to the back door and called out, "Harley, what are you doing? Why don't you come in and admire your beautiful present? Do come inside now."

Five long minutes passed, but Harley didn't walk in.

Olivia shook her head. "He's always been like this," she said, not taking her eyes off the patio, toying with the necklace in her hand.

"How did you meet Harley?" asked Madeline, to break the uncomfortable silence.

"I worked as a researcher for a couple of years at the ICC in The Hague, that's in the Netherlands by the way, but I couldn't find what I was looking for, so I moved to New York, to do more research at the UN."

To Madeline that seemed an odd reason to move all the way to New York, but then the rich are different. "What were you looking for that was so important?"

Olivia ignored the question. "I had to come to the UN," she explained as she walked along the windows in the living room, still looking out at the patio. "They have a huge collection of digitized materials from field research all over the world. I met Harley at a UN conference."

Madeline looked at her watch and curious now, said "Research on what?"

"I was working on a paper then, *The Impact of Armed Conflict on Civilian Populations*, for an academic publication," said Olivia absently, fidgeting with her necklace. "It took a month to get Harley to agree to even take my call, and even that was like pulling teeth. It was a little easier after our first meeting." She shook her head, "I wore a lot of pink back then." Olivia scanned the patio once more, "If you see Harley let me know," and she went into the hall and must have gone into a kitchen because Madeline could hear her pull pans out of a cupboard and turn on a faucet.

Olivia walked back into the living room, again to the screen door and stared out at the patio. She said to Madeline over her shoulder, "There he is, and yes, of course he's still on his damn phone. Who is he talking to that's more important than his wife on their first anniversary?" She stood by the door, watching Harley, her eyebrows knitted, the emerald necklace still in her hand. She clasped it around her neck.

Olivia looked out the door again, "Where did Harley go now? I don't see him." Then she announced, "There he is! He just walked around the corner, still talking on his phone of course."

"Well, I should be going," said Madeline, glancing down at her watch, "Happy Anniversary again. Tell Harley I'll call him later. I can see myself out. And thank you Olivia, again, I appreciate what you did. That was very courageous."

Olivia shrugged, not looking at her but watching Harley, "Think nothing of it."

"Well, goodbye then," said Madeline. As she walked back down the long hall she heard a screen door slam somewhere.

She went out the front door to her car in the driveway, the horses amiably watching her. She texted Abby that Harley had signed for the necklace and she should wire money to Sam in New York, and FedEx him the second necklace. Madeline drove down the quiet streets and was almost to the I-93 ramp when she glanced at the passenger seat and saw the bouquet of pink roses for Harley. Damn, she forgot to give them to him. She made a quick U-turn and drove back to the estate, parking in the same spot as before.

She rang the doorbell, but no one answered, and after a couple of minutes

44

she rang it again. Still no answer. As she was walking along the side of the mansion to the patio, she heard a plane overhead on a loud landing pattern into Boston's Logan Airport. A low, noisy flight path the town of Milton had been complaining about for years in *The Boston Globe*. She had to agree, the noise was jarring in the bucolic suburb.

And then, over the roar of the overhead plane she thought she heard voices, and then a sudden noise, very close. Like a bang.

* * *

Madeline turned the corner of the house seconds later, and there was Olivia standing on the edge of the patio who looked up at her in surprise. In Olivia's right hand was a gun.

Olivia stared down at the gun, and stammered," It was just lying there, on the tiles. What was it doing there?" She turned toward the path and said to Madeline, "Did you see that man? Just now? Running down to the river? In a brown shirt?" She called out, "Harley? Harley, where are you?"

"A guy in a brown shirt? No, I didn't see anyone," said Madeline, alarmed, staring at Olivia.

Olivia looked down at the gun in her hand again. "I...I just picked this up," she stammered. "Someone could accidentally kick it, and it could go off, or something." She looked around, "What on earth is going on?" Then she called out again, "Harley?" but there was no answer. Then she turned and Madeline followed her around a thick stand of trees. Then Olivia came to a dead stop.

Harley lay sprawled on his stomach under a drooping hemlock, half his body on the gray tiles, half on a small rise of the browned grass. A pool of blood was congealing along his left side.

In the middle of his back was a small circle of blood on his stark white shirt.

* * *

Olivia set the gun on a small teak table and rushed over to Harley and knelt beside him, checking his pulse as she murmured, "Oh my God, Harley?"

Madeline dropped the roses on the table, and punched in 911 on her cell phone, and an operator picked up. "There's been an accident or something," said Madeline, her voice as steady as she could make it. "Send an ambulance. I don't know what happened, but Harley Atherton, who lives here, is lying on the ground, and there's a bloody hole in the back of his shirt." A pause as Madeline was asked a question, and she replied, "He's lying face down, but he doesn't seem to be conscious." Another pause and she said, "Do you mean was he shot? I don't know. And yes, there is a gun." She listened for a moment and said, "I'm looking at it. It's on a table. And no, I don't know if there is another one. There was a man here, I didn't see him, but Harley's wife said he just ran down to the river."

She gave them Harley's address, "I'm with Harley's wife now, and we're on the patio in the back of the house. Please hurry."

"Madeline, come over here, I need to get Harley on his back yelled Olivia," as she straightened his limp arms.

Madeline came up beside her, and with three mighty heaves they rolled Harley over onto his back, and Madeline had to look away. A wide hole, the gunshot exit wound, had blasted the front of Harley's white shirt, which was soaked with blood. Olivia pulled off the scarf around her neck and pressed it against the gaping wound. She put her other hand on his neck, searching for a carotid pulse.

"Grab some towels from the bathroom, second door on the left," Olivia yelled to Madeline, who raced down the hall and came back with a stack of towels. In the meantime, Olivia had dragged Harley to a flat section of the patio and had pulled open his shirt. Olivia grabbed a towel and pressed it down hard over the jagged wound. She placed the heel of her left hand on his chest just above the bloody towel, her right hand just on top of her left and began steady chest compressions, her eyes focused on Harley's chest, her hands and her ivory sweater now covered with his blood.

Madeline began, "Is he…"

Olivia ignored her, breathlessly repeating to Harley, his eyes still closed,

"It's going to be alright Darling. It's going to be alright." She brushed back the hair on his forehead, "Don't worry, everything will be fine," the fingers of her right hand searching for his carotid artery again. And then she went back to chest compressions, the large emerald stone in her necklace swinging against her sweater.

Madeline said, "Is there anything I can do?"

Olivia shook her head and continued with her chest compressions, drops of sweat beading now on her face. She stood up abruptly, massaging her knees, grabbed another towel off the table, and with a bloody hand moved the gun away from the edge of the table. She went back to her chest compressions.

Harley's eyes were closed, his face white and drawn. The only sound was Olivia's jagged breathing.

It seemed an age before Madeline heard the sound of sirens, but it was probably only a couple of minutes, and she ran around to the front of the house. She ran back to the patio a minute later, followed by two running police officers. Olivia was still kneeling beside Harley, performing CPR. Madeline looked away.

"Is there a gun? Where is it?" shouted the first officer.

Madeline pointed to the revolver on the patio table. "There it is. At least I think that's the gun." The officer bagged it as Chase sprinted up the brick path that, she assumed, ran along the guest houses and the river. He stopped, his eyes riveted on Harley. Edgar was right behind Chase, his sharp gray eyes taking in the scene, like a cop's.

Olivia was still kneeling beside Harley watching his face as she continued with the chest compressions, and Chase knelt down beside her. He looked up at Madeline and shouted, "What happened?"

"I'm...I'm not sure."

The first officer said to Madeline, "Any other weapons?"

"I don't know. I haven't seen any."

The first police officer shouted into his phone, "It's clear," and two running EMT's, lugging medical bags, raced onto the patio, followed by a paramedic. Olivia stood up as they examined Harley, while Madeline, and Chase watched in silence as the paramedic took over CPR from Olivia. Edgar stood back from everyone, his eyes scanning the ground under the trees and shrubs on the edge of the patio.

Chase turned to Olivia, "What happened? What's going on?"

She didn't look at him, "I don't know. I think your father has been shot."

Madeline turned and watched as Edgar walked around the trees on the patio until one of the cops yelled at him, "Hey you, quit walking around and just stay put."

The paramedic checked for Harley's pulse, pulled a defibrillator out of a bag, and attached two pads to Harley. He told everyone to stand back and the machine began to whir as it searched for an erratic heartbeat.

And then, nothing. The seconds went by, but the EMT's didn't load Harley onto a gurney and siren away. They just stood there, staring down at him.

* * *

The paramedic examined the injury, and studied the pools of Harley's blood on the patio. He removed the two electrical pads from Harley's chest and looked at the two EMT's. He shook his head, then reached down and pulled a blue blanket over Harley, covering his face. The first officer quietly spoke to Olivia and tears streamed down her face. Chase looked at her, then held Harley's limp right hand in his. The second officer motioned to Madeline to follow him, and they walked several feet away.

"Is Harley dead?" she asked.

"Yes. He is deceased. I need to know who you are, and why you are here."

She explained that she'd just delivered a necklace, but she'd forgotten to leave flowers for Harley, so she'd come back with them.

"And when I walked around the corner to the patio, I saw Olivia," she ended.

"Did you hear a gun shot?"

"Yes, although I didn't know that's what it was. There was a plane flying over. Low."

"What was Mrs. Atherton doing when you walked up?" the officer asked.

"Just standing there. Surprised."

"Where was the gun?"

"In her hand," Madeline said, and stopped, realizing how that sounded, then added, "She said it must have been tossed on the patio by someone, and she'd just picked it up, so someone didn't trip on it. Or something."

The officer nodded, and asked her to describe the scene again, as a small tape recorder in his shirt pocket rolled. He motioned to the other cop, who walked over and said, "Make sure you swab everyone's hands."

The cop pulled a kit out of his bag and began to take swabs of everyone's hands, including Madeline's. Multiple sirens wailed up to the mansion, and two more uniformed officers rushed onto the patio.

"Is there a boat dock down there?" one of them yelled at Madeline.

"I have no idea."

The officer sprinted down the path and out of sight.

She glanced over at Chase and Edgar, standing by the patio door. It looked like they were arguing.

Five minutes later two officers, in the pale blue on dark blue uniform of the Massachusetts State Police walked onto the patio, and spoke to the Milton cops, who nodded and left.

"Come with me," one of the state cops said to Madeline, and he showed her and Olivia to separate state police cars. He motioned to Olivia to slide in the back seat of the first car, and had Madeline get in the one behind.

* * *

Chase and Edgar stood on the sidewalk in front of Harley's mansion, watching as Madeline and Olivia were driven away by the state police. Chase ran his hand over his forehead. His hand was cold as ice. He shivered.

"What did you see when you went outside for a cigar a couple of minutes ago?" asked Edgar.

"Nothing. I heard Dad and Olivia in the middle of an argument, so I turned around and came back. You must have been in the bedroom or something. I didn't see you."

"They were arguing? About what?"

Chase shook his head, "I don't know, I couldn't hear what he was saying, but I could tell Dad was angry, very angry. I know Olivia shot him, I just know it! She's just pretending to be upset now that he's dead. She's quite the little actress you know. I bet the police will arrest her by the end of the day, if not sooner and..."

"Look Chase, we'll just have to wait and see what the state police turn up."

"I don't want to wait." His eyes scanned the patio. "Do you know where Dad's cell phone is? It wasn't in his shirt pocket."

Edgar looked around to see if anyone was watching before he pulled a cell phone out of his pocket, "You mean this?" and he shoved it back in his pocket. "I noticed it wasn't in Harley's shirt pocket too, so I walked around until I found it. He was probably holding it when he was shot, and I figured the impact would have knocked it out of his hand." Edgar nodded towards the back of the house, "It was in the bushes, just off the patio."

Chase put out his hand, "Give it to me."

"Sorry, but no. I'll have one of my guys take a look at it. All his phones have an auto-delete function on them, so it won't do you any good. But I want to double-check anyway."

"I still want it."

"I can't give it to you. Maybe later."

"The police will just pull the cell phone records."

Edgar's smile was knowing, "Won't do them any good, since Harley buys prepaid cell phones, and then has them programmed to bounce from about ten different cell phone towers. I'm surprised you didn't know that."

They stopped talking when a state policeman walked up to them. The cop told Chase he needed to follow him to his cruiser so he could take his statement, and told Edgar to wait there because he needed his statement as well.

Chase followed the state cop to his cruiser, anxious to tell him he'd heard Harley and Olivia in an argument, a big one, right before Harley was shot.

Too bad Massachusetts didn't have the death penalty.

* * *

50

Madeline stared out the window as she was driven to the Milton barracks of the state police, at the foot of the Blue Hills Reservation. She tried to block out the image of Harley lying dead on the ground, and of Olivia covered in his blood, frantically performing CPR. When Madeline's cell phone rang she turned it on mute.

Inside the police barracks Madeline was led to a small, drab interview room, with no windows, just three chairs and a table. For well over an hour she spoke to Gregg Vanasse, a dark-haired, soft-spoken detective, explaining how she knew Harley and Olivia, why she was there, and what she saw when she came around the corner of the patio. She explained that she'd delivered an emerald necklace to Harley, left to go back to Boston, but had returned ten minutes later because she'd forgotten to give Harley a bouquet of roses.

Detective Vanasse asked her the value of the necklace, and when she told him, the cop's eyes widened but he didn't comment, all he said was, "Who knew you were delivering the necklace this afternoon?"

"Just Abby, that's my business partner, Harley, his wife and Harley's assistant Penelope."

"Tell me, what was Mrs. Atherton's demeanor when you walked around the corner?" asked the detective.

"I would say she was surprised."

"Did you see a man running down the path to the river?"

"No, but then I was only looking at Olivia, because she had a gun in her hand."

"That's the gun that was bagged by the Milton police, correct?"

"Yes."

"Whose blood is on the gun, and how did it get there?"

"It's Harley's." She explained that Olivia had been giving Harley CPR, and her hands and sweater were covered in his blood, and at one point she'd moved the pistol away from the edge of the table.

"And how was she holding this gun?"

"Holding it? Like anyone does holding a gun. It was pointed down."

Madeline repeated yet again that Olivia had asked if she'd seen a man, in brown, running down the path to the river. She said to the policeman, "I told

51

her no, I didn't see anyone, but I wasn't facing the brick path so I couldn't have seen him."

"When you saw her, did Mrs. Atherton seem uncomfortable holding the gun?"

"Uncomfortable? Hardly. I had the sense that she'd handled guns before. She seemed quite experienced."

Half an hour later Madeline was still answering questions, although they were mostly old questions and she repeated her old answers. Then another detective appeared in the doorway, and asked her, "While you were on the patio, did you hear any voices, people talking?"

She thought about it, "Well, as I was walking to the patio, I do remember hearing voices, and I think one of them was Olivia's, but I'm not sure."

"Could you hear what they were saying? Were they loud voices?"

"No, I couldn't understand what was being said. They were just voices, that's all."

The detective told her she could take a break and she sent Abby a quick text, "I'm running late."

This was not the time to let her know she'd been at the scene of a murder and was now being grilled by a homicide detective. Twenty minutes later Madeline was released, and Detective Vanasse drove her back to Harley's estate to pick up her car.

There were a couple of lights on in the mansion, and several state police vehicles parked in front. She doubted that Olivia was home yet. Madeline got in her car, took a couple of deep breaths, and pulled out her cell phone. Two texts and a phone message from Abby popped up. Madeline sent a reply to Abby's last text that she was leaving Harley's now, but it was a long story, and she'd stop by her place in Cambridge in thirty minutes. And that was it.

Madeline didn't want to tell her partner over the phone that Coda Gems' first really big customer at their new store had just been murdered. While she was there. That was more of an 'in person' type of conversation.

She put her cell phone back on mute and drove to Abby's.

* * *

Two martinis and an hour later in Cambridge she had told Abby the whole story several times.

"This is all a bit much. You deliver a $200,000 necklace to a new customer," said Abby, "and right after you leave the man is murdered? Unbelievable." She stood up and pulled shrimp and cocktail sauce out of the refrigerator, and clattered plates on the kitchen counter. "You need to eat something. So where is the necklace now?"

"Olivia, Harley's wife, was wearing it when he was shot."

"And she didn't shoot him?"

"I already told you Olivia didn't shoot Harley, she just happened to be at the wrong place at the wrong time. She knows CPR, and tried to save him."

"Do the police have a suspect?"

"They might. I don't know."

"But you are definitely not a suspect or something?"

"I am absolutely not a suspect." Madeline picked up her empty martini glass, "Do you have any Diet Coke? I have to drive home soon."

"No, you don't," said Abby, "you're staying here tonight. I insist. You were just at a murder scene and then taken to a police station for God's sake." She picked up her phone and ordered a pizza, vegetable of course.

Abby poured a glass of soda for Madeline and a glass of orange juice for herself. "Where is Olivia now?"

"I think she's still at the State Police Barracks. Or maybe she's at the Medical Examiners' office identifying the body."

Abby looked at her, eyebrows arched.

"Well, that's what happens in cop shows," said Madeline defensively. "Anyway, it's not likely they'd release her before me. There were a couple of state police cars and a van at Harley's place when I picked up my car. When Olivia is released, she'll probably have to go to a hotel, since I'm sure the house is still a crime scene. The police probably won't let her back in for at least a day or so, maybe more and..." Abby shot her a questioning look and Madeline said, "Cop shows again."

"And you said Olivia was definitely wearing the necklace?"

"Yes, I saw it around her neck after Harley had been shot."

"Well, at least we know robbery wasn't a motive for the murder. I wish you weren't involved."

"Well, there's nothing to be done about that, since I am sort of a witness."

Abby looked at Madeline, "Who do you think shot him?"

"I have no idea. It could have been anybody."

"How was Olivia when you last saw her?" asked Abby.

"Distraught but collected. Not to be too graphic, but Harley's blood was all over her hands and sweater. And it was on her slacks too." Madeline shivered.

Abby announced, "I'm going into the store first thing tomorrow morning, but you shouldn't come in. What you need are a couple of days off. As for me, I'm going to bed. You're in your usual bedroom." She gave Madeline a big hug and went upstairs.

Madeline lay awake for hours, trying to blot out the image of Harley lying on the gray tiles. And of Olivia's frantic efforts to save him.

She finally fell asleep just before 5:00 a.m.

Chapter Five

When Madeline got up, Abby was long gone to the store. After a second bagel, Madeline called Olivia's cell.

"Hey, Olivia, it's Madeline. I thought I would see how you are doing. It must be horrible for you. I am so very, very sorry about Harley. What a shocking and awful tragedy."

"Yes. I can hardly believe it. A nightmare. I didn't sleep at all last night, of course, just thinking about what I could have done. There must have been something I could have done differently."

"Well, I was there, and you did everything you possibly could. There wasn't anything else you could have done. You were totally focused on Harley and you performed CPR like an expert too and…"

"The police want to see me again later this morning," said Olivia with a sigh. "To go over the details again, I suppose."

"Is there anything I can do for you?

"No. There is nothing you or anyone can do. It is all, well it's all overwhelming," said Olivia. She didn't sound overwhelmed, she just sounded exhausted. "Last night, after the police said I could leave, Edgar drove me home so I could pack a bag. I stopped at the house to grab a few things, and a policeman had to be with me the whole time. It was gut-wrenching to walk into the house." After a pause, she continued, "Then Edgar drove me into Boston and I checked into a hotel in the Back Bay. One thing I know for sure, I won't ever spend another night at that house again. Not a single night."

"That is totally understandable."

"Madeline, actually there is something you could do. Would you be able to come to my hotel and see me for maybe fifteen or twenty minutes and talk, in a little while? If you don't mind? I'm at the Mandarin Oriental. That would be helpful since you were there when Harley was..." Olivia's voice trailed off. "I just want to make sure I remember everything," she continued. "I was in shock after it happened, and it's all still sort of a blur for me."

"Of course, and I don't mind at all. I can be there in half an hour."

"Thank you."

It was the first time Olivia had thanked her for anything.

* * *

Thirty minutes later, Madeline knocked on the door of Olivia's hotel suite in Boston's Back Bay and she opened it wide, wearing a black knit dress, with her long brown hair falling around her shoulders. She looked ten years younger. She led Madeline into a living room with a massive TV, two long sofas, and a cluster of chairs. When Olivia turned to her Madeline caught glints of an elaborate gold necklace around her neck.

"Can I get you something?" asked Olivia. "I can order anything from room service, or there's a kitchen off the living room, with a Keurig if you want coffee."

"Coffee would be good if you don't mind."

"No problem."

Madeline followed her into an alcove with gleaming, stainless steel appliances and watched as Olivia dropped a pod into the coffee maker and poured herself a tall glass of water. She led Madeline into the suite's small dining room and they sat at a black lacquer table.

"I just wish I had looked more closely at the man yesterday," said Olivia, picking up her glass, "the one who was running away. But it was all so quick. You didn't see him? You're sure? It would have been for just a couple of seconds because he was running. I really just saw a flash of movement and then he was gone."

Madeline paused, thinking, then said, "No, I didn't see anybody. So, how are you?"

56

"I'll be fine."

"Do you have any family here?"

"Family? No, I have no family." Olivia looked away.

A heavy silence, then Madeline asked, "Is Harley's son Chase helping you with the arrangements?"

"Chase? Hardly. He is the executor of Harley's estate, and he won't want to be involved in the details of the service. Chase thinks of himself as a 'big picture' kind of guy," she added with a grim smile. "Edgar told me not to worry about anything, and that he'd have Penelope come here later today to help me with decisions about Harley's..." She looked up at Madeline. "Edgar was Harley's right hand you know. Harley would get Edgar's opinion on everything."

"He's built like a professional football player. You can tell by his neck that he lifts weights."

"He probably does. Harley said he used to be a Navy SEAL and was an expert in underwater demolition. I guess he knows how to blow up things in the water, which doesn't sound all that useful but I guess it was." Olivia almost smiled. "Harley told me Edgar trained tactical teams for different clients. He depended on him."

"That's not a surprise. Edgar struck me as very capable. Anyway, if there's anything you want from the house, I can pick it up for you. That is if the police will let me inside."

"No, there's nothing I need, I'll be fine." Olivia looked away and then back to her, speaking matter-of-factly, "I feel like I'm living in a slow-motion nightmare, and now the day after our first wedding anniversary I have to plan my husband's funeral."

"How have the state police been?"

"Polite. Considerate. Lots of questions. I called this morning and spoke to a detective, but they don't have any new information. And they haven't found any other witnesses who saw a man running down the path to the Neponset. You're sure, you're absolutely positive you didn't see anyone?"

"I didn't see anyone, but then I was just looking at you. You looked like you'd seen a ghost or something."

"I was holding a gun after all," she said ruefully. "I should never have picked it up, I thought Harley had dropped it or something. He was always carrying a loaded gun around. You know he had a room just for his guns, in one of the buildings in the back. I think it was his favorite room in the whole place." She said, with a slight smile, "When we got married, I told him I had just one rule, absolutely no guns in the house. Which by the way, was a rule he ignored."

She continued, "The police have identified the gun, and it was one of Harley's. It did make me crazy that he always carried a gun. He said it was a habit, from his days as an Army Ranger. He must have set it down somewhere when he was on the patio talking on the phone, and the police said the 'perp,' that's what they call a murderer I guess, could have just picked it up. Olivia shook her head. "I told him always carrying a gun was a habit he needed to break." A tear rolled down her face. "If only he had."

"What about security cameras? Were there any on the patio?"

"We'd just extended the living room and put in all new windows. They had to be custom-made of course because they were so huge, but then that's Harley. Anyway, the exterior cameras hadn't been mounted yet. So no, no cameras in the back. All the doors and windows are alarmed of course, and they all have cameras, just not in the back."

Olivia sat composed, her hands in her lap, "After you left yesterday, I waited for Harley in the living room, and then when he still hadn't come in, I went outside to find him. He was standing just under the trees, and we talked for a couple of minutes, and I showed him the necklace. He told me it was beautiful and of course, I told him again how much I loved it, and that I loved him for giving it to me because it was exactly what I wanted.

"I think I remember a plane flying over our house, coming in to land at Logan. To be honest I barely notice them anymore. Anyway, as he and I were talking I remembered I had a tray of appetizers in the oven that were likely burning, so I turned away and started back to the house when I heard a loud noise, and another sound...or something, sort of a thud, I can't really remember." She shivered, "and then I saw a glint of metal on the patio. It was a gun, and I...I picked it up. I don't know why I did. I remember thinking 'what in God's name is that doing here?' And then I heard someone running and looked up. Like I said, it was just a glimpse. Then you came around the corner." Olivia finished her glass of water and poured another from the carafe. Olivia stared down at her hands and then up at Madeline. "I've been going over and over everything in my mind ever since. Wondering if I missed anything. The police had so many questions." She sighed, "What kind of questions did they ask you?"

"Just why I was there, and what I saw. I told them how you tried to save Harley with CPR, and…"

"You told them I was holding a gun," she said.

"I did, and that you'd said it was lying on the ground and you'd just picked it up."

"Which was exactly what I told them. They asked me if I had a gun license, and I said no, that I'd never had a gun in my hand before. I am also a big supporter of tighter gun control laws." She added with a sad smile, "That was about the only thing Harley and I didn't agree on."

Madeline paused, remembering she'd told the detective she thought Olivia had handled guns before, and she seemed "quite experienced." Madeline wasn't about to mention that comment to Olivia. Madeline decided there were times she definitely talked too much.

In the silence, Olivia brushed her hair back with both hands, and Madeline could clearly see the elaborate gold necklace around her neck. It was a classic piece of traditional North African jewelry, Berber as she recalled. Not usually worn as a necklace, it had gold pendants inset with diamonds that hung from the 24-kt. filigree gold chain.

"That is a fabulous khit errouh piece," commented Madeline, nodding toward the necklace.

Startled, Olivia said, "This? Is that what it's called? It is unusual, isn't it? It's one of the few things I grabbed besides some clothes when I was in the house last night. My mother gave it to me. It's Algerian." Olivia patted the elaborate gold and diamond necklace. Traditionally, it's worn across the forehead but I had a jeweler make some adjustments. It's quite valuable."

"It's an amazing piece." Madeline leaned forward to look at it. "I've read about them, but I've only ever seen photos, never the real thing. It's very striking and—"

"I'll be back in a minute," interrupted Olivia, and walked out of the small dining room. When she came back, she had taken off the khit errouh piece and now had the emerald necklace from Harley around her neck. The overhead light caught the marquis-cut edges of the emerald stone, and it glittered.

Olivia said, "It is gorgeous, isn't it? Harley has…had…good taste." With a small smile, she added,"Well, actually, I was the one with the good taste." She checked her watch. "I'm not looking forward to talking to the police again. It's all a bit much because to be honest, I feel like I'm a suspect or something."

Madeline didn't think it would be helpful if she pointed out to Olivia that she most likely was, so she didn't. Instead, she said, "I have a friend, Donia, who used to be a homicide detective with the Boston Police. She probably knows the homicide detectives with the state police in Milton. I can ask her if she can make a call or two to them and see what she can find out."

"You would do that for me?" and Olivia straightened in her chair. "I would really appreciate it if you did. That would be very helpful."

"Olivia, of course, I'll help you. I owe you for what you did."

Olivia acknowledged the comment with a flash of a smile. "Don't worry about that. I don't know how much longer the house will be a crime scene, not long, I hope. I'm waiting for the police to let me have movers get inside. I'll have them pack up my things and ship them to…I don't know where yet, somewhere. I'm not sure where I'll go. Somewhere safe though. I just want to be done with that house, for forever."

Olivia looked exhausted, so Madeline stood up, and Olivia stood as well. At that moment the sun came out from behind a heavy, dark cloud, and Madeline looked at Olivia, as a slender ray of sunlight played across her calm, stoic face.

Olivia glanced down at her emerald necklace, "I loved this from the second I saw it. It reminds me of one my mother had a long time ago, hers had a big emerald pendant too, very much like this one. She would wear it to opening nights or to state dinners, or to swank parties, the kind with waiters in white tuxes.

"She had matching emerald earrings too, tear-drop ones. There must have been at least four carats in each one. She looked so beautiful with her brown hair swept up, glittering in her emeralds," Olivia's voice softened with reverie.

"Sounds like she was very glamorous," said Madeline.

"Yes, she was drop-dead glamorous. My mother told me once when I was a little girl that her emeralds would be mine one day, along with everything else. But that didn't happen. None of it happened." Olivia ran her fingers along the emerald stone and continued, as she stared unseeingly out the window. "I was an heiress once of a fortune, a very large fortune, but that was a long time ago, in another world," and she turned to Madeline as a sadness stole across her face. "That world doesn't exist anymore, at least not for me."

Madeline shifted uncomfortably, not sure what to say. "I am sorry to hear that."

"Anyway, it was good of you to come," Olivia said, "I've been feeling very alone." She took Madeline's hand and they stood silently for several minutes watching the sky as dark thunder clouds moved in. It would rain soon.

At the door, Madeline leaned forward to kiss Olivia goodbye on the cheek and she left. Someone needed to care about what would happen to Olivia.

That someone would be her.

* * *

Chase sat in Harley's office at Atherton Global. It seemed strange to be sitting in his father's Italian leather office chair. Harley would never let anyone else sit in it, and he had told Chase once it cost $10,000. The chair was high-backed, with padded arms, footrest, and a lever that could tilt and swivel the back and arms in fifteen different angles, including fully reclined. Chase leaned back in the chair, which was worth every penny he thought, and then he saw Edgar in the doorway. Chase stood up, saying, "Let's go outside and get some fresh air."

Edgar followed him down the corridor to the elevator and then out to

State Street, and its bumper-to-bumper, angry traffic.

"Sorry," said Chase, "but I know my dad's office is wired and everything is recorded. I'm having it swept this afternoon, and until then, I just want to be careful. The cops might be listening." They crossed the street, and Chase said, "Do you know why Dad went to Paris last week?"

Edgar shook his head. "He never said. Even Penelope didn't know, and Olivia doesn't know either, because she asked me. So no one knows."

Chase said, "That's too bad. I called the state police this morning and spoke to one of their detectives. I thought for sure Olivia would be arrested and charged with Dad's murder by now. After all, she did have the gun in her hand; can't get much more incriminating than that can it? I know she did it, I just know she shot him. I've never trusted her. Did you know Dad had just put a tap on Olivia's phone a couple of hours before he was shot?"

"He did? So what was on it?"

Chase looked at Edgar, who hadn't asked why his father was tapping Olivia's phone, he wanted to know what the tap had turned up. Which was interesting, so Chase asked him, "Why did Dad do that? Have her phone tapped I mean."

"I have no idea. So, what was on the phone tap?"

Chase said, "It was just Olivia talking to that jeweler, that blonde woman, Madeline. The two of them seemed quite chummy like they've been best friends for a long time."

Chase was not about to tell Edgar what he'd heard when he'd listened to the phone call between the two women just a couple of hours before Harley's murder. Chase had listened over and over to Olivia saying to Madeline, "Like I said, though, don't say a word to Harley about yesterday. Not a single word. I told you he sees conspiracies everywhere, so I have to be very careful, about everything. Very careful. Especially today."

It was clear to Chase that Olivia had concocted a secret plan, and Madeline was in on it. He saved the recording. He knew it wouldn't be admissible at Olivia's trial because it had been illegally recorded, but with any luck, he'd find another use for it.

Chase continued, "I know Olivia put pressure on Dad to buy the damn emerald necklace because he told me that last night. He finally gave in and agreed to buy it, then today this Madeline woman delivers it, leaves, and ten minutes later she sneaks back to our patio. And then 'boom' Dad is dead. I'd like to know more about this Madeline woman and find out what she's really up to. I think she knows things. I'll have to get her to talk."

"And how will you do that? Tie her up and shine bright lights in her eyes? Is that what you learned when you were at M.I.T.? Funny, I thought it was a school for geeks."

Chase ignored Edgar, biting his words. "You know what I want? I want Olivia to go to prison for Murder One. I don't want her to weasel out of it with some kind of 'candy-ass' second-degree murder charge, or a ridiculous manslaughter one. I want Murder One, the kind with no chance of parole for the first twenty-five years. And bringing a conspiracy charge into the investigation could seal the deal."

"You're a criminal investigator now?" said Edgar, all but laughing.

Chase felt his face flush. Edgar was a stereotypical, 'shoot 'em up,' gung-ho type. Harley had never bothered to hide his preference for the swashbuckling Edgar, the son he probably wished he'd had.

"I'll see what else besides Harley's cell phone I can turn up," said Edgar. "I'd like to get into the crime scene, have another look around, but that's not going to happen."

Chase looked at him, "So you know something?"

Edgar shook his head, "Nothing concrete really. Just things that don't add up. Odd things."

"Like what?"

Edgar checked his watch, "Sorry, but I have to leave." He didn't sound sorry. "I've got an appointment," and he nodded to Chase and set off down the street.

Chase went back inside 60 State Street and up to the executive floor of Atherton Global to Harley's office, or rather *his* office now. He picked up the phone and called the state police for an update on Harley's investigation. Chase wasn't about to sit around and wait for them to call him. He needed to know what they were up to, and when they'd be arresting Olivia. He wanted her behind bars as soon as possible.

* * *

After Madeline left Olivia's hotel, she called Donia on her way back to Abby's house. Donia was the head of security at the Isabel Stewart Gardner Museum in Boston, but before that, she had been a homicide detective with the Boston Police Department.

When Donia picked up the phone Madeline said, "It's me, Madeline. Can we get together? I need your opinion."

"Sure, I have lots of opinions. What kind do you want?"

"Let's go with one on homicide charges. It's a long story." She checked her watch. "I don't know when you'll be leaving work, but can I meet you for a drink at six? How about Woody's, on Hemenway Street in the Fenway?"

"Well, yes, I can do that. Besides, I haven't talked to you in an age."

* * *

When Madeline walked into Woody's, Donia was standing inside the door, waiting for a table. Tall and slender, in her mid-thirties, Donia was in slacks and a sweater, her brown hair, as usual, pulled back. She walked like a ballet dancer; taut, studied, and precise. A waiter led them to a table in the back.

Madeline had met Donia last winter, when Donia was still a homicide detective, investigating the murder of a customer of Madeline's, a very wealthy widow. A homicide case that was never solved, and likely to remain so for lack of evidence. The problem for Donia was that Madeline knew who the murderer was, and Donia knew that she knew. But Madeline refused to tell her. Donia hated cold cases, especially ones that had happened on her watch.

"I am surprised you aren't all that anxious to see the killer brought to justice," Donia had told her before, about five times. Madeline got tired of hearing that, and one night said to her, "Just stop it, alright? Don't worry about it, Donia. I keep telling you that you'll have to trust me on this one.

64

Justice has been served."

Donia never brought it up again, but Madeline knew she hadn't forgotten.

That afternoon Madeline set her purse on a booth in the back and slid on the worn bench, saying, "Well, you're not going to believe this, but I'm sort of involved in a homicide investigation, and…"

"Homicide? Is it the widow's murder, because I'd really like to know who…"

"No, not that one. A couple of days ago a guy by the name of Harley Atherton was murdered in Milton."

Donia said, "Harley Atherton, from Milton?"

Madeline nodded.

"I know the name," said Donia. "The man was worth about a billion dollars. Seriously, that's his net worth. His wife died very suddenly in the middle of what I was told was a very ugly divorce a couple of years ago. Since it was an 'unattended death,' meaning no one was with her, it was reported to the coroner, who brought in her primary care doctor to get the death certificate signed. As it turned out she died of natural causes, a cardiac aneurysm, sudden and quick."

"Well, that's sad," said Madeline. "Anyway, I'm guessing the state police are about to charge his current wife, Olivia with Harley's murder. I know she didn't do it, and I'm afraid she'll be railroaded into a prison sentence with basically just circumstantial evidence. He was shot, in the middle of the day."

"He was shot? asked Donia, and Madeline nodded. "Any witnesses?" continued Donia.

"Sort of."

"What do you mean?"

"Well, I think the cops have already jumped to the conclusion that his wife did it. Cops make snap judgments all the time, and then they stick with them. And, well, the witness at the scene saw Olivia, the wife, holding the gun that killed him less than a minute after it happened." Madeline arched her eyebrows, "That witness would be me. Olivia told me she'd just found the gun on the patio, didn't know what it was doing there, and so she picked it up. And that's when I walked in. She called out Harley's name, then she and I walked around the corner, and there he was, lying on the ground with a bullet in his back."

"So you are 'in the soup' again," said Donia matter-of-factly.

"Yes. And if there is a trial, I'll have to testify."

"Absolutely."

Madeline fidgeted in her seat "I don't want to do that. I don't want to do that at all. I will feel horrible because my testimony will be very damaging to his wife."

"You don't have a choice about testifying. You'll be slapped with a subpoena if you refuse."

"The police seem focused on her. Only on her, I may add."

"If they want you to testify, you'll have to. That's it, end of story. It sounds like she's their only suspect?"

"That's the problem, which is why I have to help her."

"Madeline, why in God's name are you involved in this? I don't mean as a witness, it sounds to me like you intend to investigate a murder. Why?"

"Not investigate, just come up with real suspects. My testimony can be spun by the prosecutor as the key piece of evidence that sends her to prison. It's true that I did see her holding the gun that killed him less than a minute or so after he was shot, but that certainly doesn't mean she shot him. I owe her for something very brave she did for me."

"Well, it must have been something very big," said Donia, waiting for Madeline to continue.

"It's a long story. I just don't believe Olivia killed her husband," said Madeline.

"Well, then, who did shoot him?"

"I have no idea. All I want is for the police to shift their attention off Olivia, and find the real murderer. I would think there's a lot of people who'd have a good reason to kill Harley since he was a private military contractor after all."

"Well, she'd probably appreciate your support in other ways."

"Really, like what, handing her a hankie?" said Madeline, a little too loudly because several customers at the bar looked over at her. "Anyway, I am hoping that you could find out what the police are thinking? You know, get a sense of where they are with their investigation?" continued Madeline. "I'm assuming you know some of the state police detectives out of the Milton barracks."

"I do."

"So maybe you could sort of ask them about the case. Just generally, you know what I mean? I want to know if they're seriously looking at other suspects. That's all. I just want to keep Olivia from being arrested."

"I am a security professional, not a blabber-mouth busybody. I couldn't do that."

"Why? You're not on the Boston Police force anymore."

"Doesn't matter. I'd help you if I could, but I absolutely will not pry info out of any detective in an ongoing investigation for you. That would be unethical. Besides, they wouldn't tell me anyway. I can't believe you're getting involved in this. Who do you think you are, Nancy Drew?"

"No. Annie Oakley."

"She was a sharpshooter, not a detective."

"So you won't help me?"

"No, I just can't do that, and I am sorry. I would if I could, but I can't do what you want."

"Understood," said Madeline, "I guess."

"Exactly how, do you intend on going about finding these murder suspects?"

"I have no idea."

It's a good thing you don't have a gun," Donia said as she looked around the crowded bar for a waiter.

"Speaking of which, I will. I am in the process of getting a license, the concealed carry kind. I took a class at a gun range a couple of days ago, and big surprise, the instructor told me I have a natural ability. He also said it's good that I'm not afraid of guns."

"That is not what I would exactly call a talent," Donia said, turning back to Madeline.

Madeline shrugged. "Whatever. Once my license arrives, I'll have a blown-up print of it made, then frame it in something expensive of course, and hang it in the store. Next to our Boston Symphony prints."

"Tell me again, why are we friends?" sighed Donia.

"Because I am a fascinating, trustworthy, and loyal person. Who is hoping that a friend, that would be you, will help her."

Donia laughed, "Just leave it to the professionals, you'll only be in the way. My advice is to stay out of it. Totally out of it."

"I can't, I have to do something. Anyway, I'm going to buy a gun as soon as I have a license. I should have a gun. Every woman needs a reliable timepiece, and a gun."

"Now I really need a drink. Where is a waiter?"

* * *

The next morning, when Abby walked in the door of Coda Gems at 8:59, Madeline told her she'd be in late the next day.

"I'm going to Harley's service tomorrow morning."

"Why? You're not related, and you weren't friends. Plus, you barely knew him," said Abby.

"You make it sound ghoulish."

"It sounds ghoulish because it is."

"I'm not going to the actual funeral, just to the wake."

"Same thing, more or less. Well, I'm not going with you." Abby opened the refrigerator door and shoved a brown bag with her lunch inside.

"I didn't ask you to."

"Good. Because I think it's weird."

Madeline sighed, "I feel like I have to go, for Olivia, because I was there right after Harley was shot, and well, that day that I...tripped on Newbury Street? I told you about that. Anyway, she saved me from getting killed by a car. She could have been killed too, or at least seriously hurt. So I do owe her."

"So go then, and I'm grateful she saved your life. But just don't tell me about Harley's service when you come back. I don't want to hear a word about it."

"No problem," said Madeline. "You don't need to be so touchy."

"Tell me, why should I be 'touchy' about the fact that my business partner is, *yet again* may I point out, somewhat, even if this time it's peripherally involved in a murder investigation? It's just not normal."

Abby shook her head and went to her desk.

* * *

Madeline called Olivia in the afternoon because she couldn't stop thinking about her, and she was worried. "Hey, Olivia, I'm just checking in. How did it go when you talked to the police?"

"They had questions about a guy who used to work for Harley a long time ago. Wallace something or other, from Boston. I guess he was killed in a hunting accident in New Hampshire last week."

"Wallace Wright, the guy from Raytheon? He used to work for Harley?" said Madeline, surprised. "It made the headlines in *The Globe*."

"So you read about it then? Anyway, I know nothing about the man. Harley knew a lot of people, and he may have mentioned him, I suppose. I'm pretty sure I never met him. I could have because I went with Harley to a lot of business dinners, but I don't remember him."

"I'm surprised the police brought that up."

"I thought so too. But they're probably just being thorough."

"Probably. Have they found anybody else who saw the guy running down to the river after Harley was shot?"

"No. No one else saw anyone, as far as I know. And nobody noticed a boat or anything pulled up to the dock that afternoon. For all I know they could have swum up to the dock. Like I said, I just caught a glimpse, and after I talked to the investigator for an hour about that, he made me realize that, well, that it might not have been a man. That it could have been a woman. So I guess that is progress."

Madeline didn't think it sounded like much progress, since whatever the gender, there still wasn't anyone besides Olivia who had seen him. Or her.

Chapter Six

The next morning, Madeline left early for Harley's wake, which was scheduled for 10:00, an hour before his funeral service. The ceremony was to be held at the Cathedral of the Holy Cross, a massive Gothic church that took up an entire city block in South Boston. The cathedral had been built over 160 years ago when Boston Catholics went to Mass every Sunday, and a good number even during the week. These days its parishioners mostly went to Mass on Christmas and Easter, or so Madeline had read. She didn't go even then.

Madeline stood outside the cathedral, and for the next thirty minutes, no one walked up the steps. Then a string of shiny black limousines began to pull up, and soberly dressed men in dark suits got out, looking neither to the right nor the left as they headed up the stairs into the cathedral and disappeared inside. Madeline guessed they were Harley's contractors. They all had the look and the haircuts of ex-military. And now that she thought about it, they were all probably armed.

She also noticed several men in the blue uniform of the Massachusetts State Police standing on the bottom steps, scanning the mourners. They were definitely armed. Now that she was in the process of becoming a gun owner, she thought about things like that.

Madeline went inside, through a dark foyer and into the church proper, where over a hundred mourners were clustered at the front. She saw Olivia, who must have come in by a side door, standing next to Harley's dark gray casket. She wore a midnight-black dress, the emerald necklace around her neck, talking to several men in suits. Olivia saw Madeline and walked up to her.

"How kind of you to come," she said.

"I wanted to be here, for you. How are you?"

"All right, thank you." She glanced out at the mourners. "Just curious, did you have a chance to talk to your ex-cop friend? About how the state police are proceeding with their investigation?"

"I did. I've been meaning to tell you she can't talk to the state police about Harley's case. She said it would be unethical."

Olivia frowned. "That's too bad. I was hoping you'd have something for me. I need all the help I can get. The police showed up yesterday with a search warrant and took my laptop, so I had to run out and get another one. They made me nervous."

She gripped Madeline's hand for a second and turned and walked over to a man in a long, brown robe, with a red hat on his graying hair. No less than Boston's cardinal was officiating. The Catholic Church was pulling out all the stops for Harley. He must have been a big donor.

Madeline scanned the mourners, and out of the corner of her eye saw Penelope walking down the aisle to the front of the cathedral. The woman was all in black, except for a pink silk scarf around her neck, a pale pink, but definitely still in the pink family. Even from a distance, she saw that Penelope's eyes were red and swollen. She saw Madeline and walked over to her.

"Hello, Madeline. How awful. Isn't it awful? I can't believe it. I can hardly believe it."

"Yes, it is a shock. I am sad for you."

"I've known Harley for thirty-six years. A lifetime, really. I was in my early twenties you know when I started working for him." She looked at Madeline. "He was always so sweet to me. I will miss him dreadfully." Penelope looked away and then down at her hands, as a tear slowly slipped down her cheek. "If only…" and she stopped. "I could tell his mood you know with just one look. Harley was a good man, who made one or two bad decisions in his life. That doesn't cancel out the good, does it?"

And Penelope looked so beseechingly into her eyes that Madeline said,

"Absolutely not."

Penelope turned and gazed at Harley's casket and said in a small voice, "It makes me sad that I will never see him walk through the door again."

"He was… an unusual person." Nice and tactful thought Madeline, and she smiled at Penelope.

"You know years ago he used to have pink roses sent to me every week, on a Friday," said Penelope. "Even when he was out of the country. He knew I loved pink." She stopped abruptly as if she'd said too much.

She had. Madeline looked at her. So, the relationship had once been more than employer-employee. A long time ago.

Penelope looked at her watch, the silver Patek she'd just bought from Madeline. "Well, I need to check in with Cardinal Marley and make sure everything is on schedule. He's very strict about schedules. It was nice to see you again Madeline." She pulled a small notebook out of her bag and hurried away.

* * *

Madeline looked around at the mourners in the church, standing in small clusters, speaking in low tones. She didn't know anyone else, except for Chase and Edgar, standing off to the side, talking. Good, she'd stop and speak to Chase for a minute.

As she walked up to him, his back to her, she heard him saying to Edgar, "..and I asked the cops about a connection with Wallace's death and Dad's, but they've decided there's nothing there. Just in case I checked around and found an old box of files from Wallace's time tucked away in Dad's back office so I took it home."

"Do *not* tell the cops you have it. You should take it and—" interrupted Edgar. He stopped when he saw Madeline and nodded to Chase. Chase turned and faced her.

She said, "Hello, Chase. My sympathies for your loss. It is all such an awful shock. I am so sorry."

"Thank you for coming to Dad's service, I appreciate it." He gave her a quick smile and was about to turn back to Edgar.

Madeline wanted to say something more than the standard words of sympathy to Chase, so she added, "I hope you'll be able to take some time off." He stared at her blankly and she continued, "To grieve, you know, since it was so sudden." Well, that was clumsy.

"Yes, yes it was tragic and sudden. I'll be spending a couple of days on the Cape, at Dad's place in Chatham, to grieve."

He nodded to her and turned back to Edgar. Madeline walked away, feeling like she was at an awkward cocktail party, except for the body of a murdered man in a casket the color of a gun twenty feet away. Abby was right, she shouldn't have come.

Several more mourners filed in and she thought she'd stand around looking sad for a bit, and then she would leave. She would definitely not stay for the actual funeral service. She saw Olivia talking to Edgar and didn't want to interrupt, so after a couple of minutes she left.

On her way down the front steps, she noticed three state police cars parked a discreet block away. The police usually did attend the last rites of a murder victim, to see who showed up, and who didn't. At the foot of the steps was a crush of limos parked behind the glossy hearse waiting for the mourners. She did feel a twinge of guilt that she hadn't thought once about Harley at his wake, much less her own mortality, which was supposedly one of the purposes of funerals. She just hadn't felt like it.

What she did feel like doing was getting on her laptop right away. She was intrigued by the thought there just might be a possible connection between Wallace's hunting death and Harley's murder. Maybe the New Hampshire state police hadn't looked hard enough. If there was a connection that would certainly shift the state police focus off Olivia and give them something real to investigate. Another good part was she wouldn't get in the way of the police investigation since they weren't checking into it. Which would make Donia, her prickly, ex-cop friend happy, if she knew about it. Which she wouldn't because Madeline was not about to mention it.

Yes, at the very least checking into Wallace's death and any possible connection with Atherton Global was something she could do for Olivia. All

73

Madeline would have to do was follow up on that shooting. Yes, that was something meaningful she could do. She never had been the hankie type anyway.

* * *

When Madeline walked into the store half an hour later, five customers were there, peering in their glass cases and talking. Abby glanced at her as she waited on one of them and muttered to Madeline as she walked past, "It's about time."

During a lull at the store, Madeline googled Wallace Wright's obituary, but it didn't go past his Raytheon years so there was no mention of Atherton Global. She kept up her internet search in between customers but didn't find anything more.

Then, at home after work, she was able to spend some uninterrupted time on her laptop and found what she'd been looking for in an old news article. Wallace had worked for Atherton Global from 1999 to 2002 as Chief Financial Officer. So, there was a business connection, but that was all the information she could find. As she was staring at her computer, she thought of Penelope, who'd said she'd worked for Harley for thirty-six years. Yes, Penelope would have known Wallace, and there was a chance she knew about a box of old files in Harley's back office. Maybe she'd even been the one to secret them there.

Madeline called Atherton Global and asked for her, but the receptionist said she was taking some time off and wasn't sure when she would return. Which was frustrating, but not a surprise. Madeline drummed her fingers on her desk. She did have to do something to help Olivia, she couldn't just sit around while the police were closing in on her with a murder charge in their pockets. The problem was, she couldn't think of anything.

* * *

The next day, as Madeline was reading *The Boston Globe*, she saw Felix's name

74

in a short blurb on the front page, announcing he had re-joined their Pulitzer-Prize Winning Spotlight Team as a senior investigative reporter. Which she knew was going to happen. What she didn't know was that according to the blurb, his first assignment would be a Spotlight series on gun-related deaths in New England. Well, that was good, that should keep him busy since he'd throw himself into investigating that politically explosive issue with his usual total and relentless absorption.

And then she smiled because this also meant Felix might be interested in Harley's murder. After all, Harley had been up to his neck in guns his whole life. So yes, Felix could be very interested, and very helpful. Very helpful. Unfortunately, the last time she'd seen him she'd basically said she wanted nothing to do with him again. Ever. Which was a problem since she couldn't just pick up the phone and give him a call out of the blue.

However, he had recited Lauren Bacall's famous whistle line, "If you want me just whistle," as he was leaving her condo that night, which could have been to salve his ego. But at least it meant he didn't totally hate her. 'Totally' was too strong a word, how about 'Maybe'? Or even 'Probably'? And then she came up with another word, 'Likely,' which sounded much better.

So she called him.

He answered with, "What's up, Madeline?" in his 'I'm really very busy right now' tone she knew so well.

She began, "Congratulations, I just read about your new Spotlight series on gun-related deaths in New England."

"If you've shot someone lately in New England, I'm very interested."

"I haven't. But I am sort of involved in one, maybe even two, gun deaths. I guess you could say I'm in the 'Murder Business.'"

"Why does that not surprise me?" A silence, then voices. Someone must have walked into his office, because he said, "Sorry, I have to go, but I'll call you back later." And he hung up.

Madeline knew he would call her back, it was the word 'later' that was a problem. It could be a couple of days or even a week before he got back to her. She gave him ten minutes and called him back.

This time he answered with, "It must be important."

"It is," and she told him about the shooting of a Raytheon executive in New Hampshire, and about Harley Atherton, her customer, who was murdered while she was at his home. She also told him the two men had known each other. She continued, "So, I don't know, maybe somebody is gunning down people who work or used to work for Atherton Global? They're a private military company, you know, like Eric Prince's Blackwater company, and Harley's contractors are accustomed to shooting people and—"

He interrupted, "I know that Harley Atherton was shot, of course, since it is big news. But you were there, at his place in Milton, when he was shot and killed?"

"Yes. Although I didn't see it happen, I was walking around the back of his house when he was shot. About a minute or so later I saw his wife, holding the gun. She didn't shoot him by the way, she'd just picked the gun up on the patio tiles. The guy who did it ran off. Just so you know, I have no idea who that was."

There was a long silence before Felix said, "I have two thoughts, the first is that you seem to have an unsettling ability to attract murder, which I'm sure has occurred to you, and the second is, why are you telling me this?"

"Because I know his wife, who is a suspect, and I don't believe she did it. So, I thought I'd check into it, and I thought you might be interested in the case since you are now investigating New England gun deaths."

"You called me hoping that I can dig up information for you?" Felix's voice was flat, emotionless. Probably because she'd made it clear when she'd last seen him that while he was interested in a relationship she was not, which most people, well make that mostly all, don't like to hear.

"I was thinking..." she began.

"You called me for help because it's something you can't find out yourself. I think you should find somebody else for that. I'm busy."

"I'm sorry, I shouldn't have called." A pause, then, "maybe you are right, a little bit right."

He sighed, and there was a silence. She had to do something fast since he would no doubt hang up on her any second. She couldn't exactly blame him either, so she started to whistle, not just any tune but the French National

Anthem, a nod to *Casablanca's* big bar scene with the Nazis. Madeline was sure he'd remember it, he probably could even recite Bogart's dialog.

After five bars he was laughing and said, "You whistled in the wrong key, it should be G Major." Felix was a big opera buff too and knew his way around the music scale. Regardless, it was a good sign that he was still talking to her. His heart indeed still did beat for a story, and he was at least somewhat intrigued with hers.

She quickly added, "By the way, the whistle part, that was a joke. I didn't mean—"

He laughed again, said he'd get back to her shortly and disconnected.

* * *

Madeline thought back four years ago to one of her last conversations with Felix when they were still married. He'd walked in the door at 10:30 pm that night, which wasn't unusual. In the evenings he was usually meeting with a source, prying more information out of a cooperative source, or hunting for a new one. He'd said once it took about five years to establish a good relationship with a trustworthy source. He'd called them his 'lifeblood.'

She remembered Felix had shut their front door behind him, his face etched with exhaustion. Too bad, she'd thought, and had said to him, her voice bitter, "If I were one of your damned sources, or even better, a whistleblower, you'd pay more attention to me."

He'd kissed her on the lips and set his computer bag on the floor. "I'm so sorry, I got hung up and couldn't call. And just so you know, most whistleblowers are men. A lot of them aggrieved men with an axe to grind, but thank God for them."

He took his laptop out of his bag and went to his study. She went back to her book, a thriller that didn't thrill, and then she'd gone to bed. An hour later Felix crawled into bed beside her and put his arms around her. She pretended to be asleep. Felix was leaving shortly for Moscow, to work on yet another ground-breaking expose. And she was upset about it. Again. God knew how long he'd be gone this time.

He did leave for Moscow two days later, and after a week he called to let her know that he'd have to "stay in Moscow for another two or three weeks. Maybe more. I'll let you know."

Which sparked yet another acrimonious argument, and after fifteen minutes she'd hung up.

She'd set up a meeting with a lawyer the next day, and three months later they were officially divorced. He then moved to Chicago and Felix was out of her life for three years. However, now he was back in her life, more or less. Mostly less.

* * *

Felix did call her back thirty minutes later, and she told him she was checking into the possibility of a connection between the shooting death of Raytheon's Wallace Wright with Harley's murder.

"They were sort of in the same business since they both had the military and law enforcement as big clients. More than twenty years ago though they actually worked together for a couple of years, at Harley's company. So there might be a connection."

"A connection?" he said. "You call that a connection? If they worked together over twenty years ago I'd call that connection a stretch, a very big stretch. Let me think about it, and I'll see what I can come up with. And you know, I'd like to talk to the widow, since I might be able to use part of her story in one of my pieces. It's called tit-for-tat. I give you something and you give me something."

"Olivia? She can't help, since she knows nothing about Wallace. She never met him, or at least doesn't remember ever meeting him."

"So, this is a wild goose chase," he said. "You seem to be under the misapprehension that I'm a 'wild goose hunter.'"

"Well, you are. In a good way of course. I'll check into setting you up with Olivia. It's not a wild goose chase."

"Good, because I don't hunt birds," he said and hung up.

Felix called her back two hours later. "I can't believe I did this for you," he began, "but I talked to a guy I know with the New Hampshire State Police. He tried to be helpful, but they basically don't have any hard evidence that points to anything other than an accidental shooting of this Wright guy by a person or persons unknown. There were two others in his hunting party, but neither they nor their guns were involved. Anyway, the police were able to figure out the approximate spot the shooter fired the gun, but no shell casing or footprints were found. No nothing. It appeared as if it had been cleaned of any evidence. What isn't in question is that the shooter was a crack shot, and careful. It happened north of Deerfield, which is a pretty isolated area. The police did a good amount of legwork and talked to the locals, but nobody else was seen in the area around that time, except for two brothers who live a mile away who don't own guns, or hunt, and some woman with a camera taking pictures. They are still actively working the case, but they don't have a single lead. It may well end up classified as 'accidental'. That's it, that's all I've got. I wasn't able to get anything else for you. There seems to be zero connection with this Harley's murder. Not a thing."

"Oh," she said, disappointed. "Well, I appreciate your checking into it. Really, I do. Thank you."

"Appreciation appreciated. Sorry it didn't work out, but thank you for thinking of me."

That was a business-like way of firmly ending a conversation. She wasn't used to that from Felix. She didn't like it and didn't want the conversation to end there.

"I was so hoping the New Hampshire cops would have turned up something, well, concrete," she said. She wanted to give Olivia some information that might be helpful.

"Well, the police don't have anything. I got all the information they have about that shooting. But I did do some background checking on your dead guy from Milton, Harley Atherton. Because well, I find him pretty interesting. By the way, I don't know if you're aware of this, but the guy has a net worth of a billion dollars."

Madeline laughed, "He does? He really does? Maybe that's why he and his son are both jerks."

"Could be. Anyway, Harley and his company were mixed up with some, shall we say dangerous characters from North Africa about twenty years ago, when Harley lived in Miami. It seems he was up to his neck in training and arming both sides in armed conflicts, not at the same time of course; Libya, Morocco, Algeria, Tunisia, you name it. A couple of them he was a little bit involved, but much more so in others. I'm trying to figure out a way to use that in my Spotlight series."

"Fascinating," said Madeline. Well, it was, sort of. She had to be nice to Felix since he was a good person to know. All she wanted was to find a solid connection between Wallace's murder and Harley's and then turn it over to the police, and there wasn't anyone else she knew who could help her.

"Back then Harley had some seriously bad people as clients," said Felix.

"Could be," said Madeline absently, looking at her nails. She needed to make an appointment for a manicure.

"You shouldn't be involved in this."

Tuesday would be good she thought.

"Are you paying attention?"

"Absolutely. What's next?"

"What do you mean what's next? I have to admit though that I am just a bit curious about this case, and I just might be able to use some of it in my series since he was after all shot in Milton. I'll let you know if I find anything."

"It is an interesting one isn't it?"

"By the way, I was wondering, where did the gun come from that was used to shoot this Harley guy?"

"It was his. His wife said he had a special room just for guns in one of the buildings in the back. There's a horse barn too, and a couple of horses."

"That's interesting. I'd like to get a couple of photos of this gun room. And like I told you, I'd like to talk to the wife, in case I can use her story."

"Well, this really isn't a good time for that. I think..."

"That was part of the deal, I help you, and you help me."

"Of course," she said, thinking quickly, "I just meant I can't do it right away. Her husband was just buried yesterday."

"Sorry, I didn't know that. It would be great though if you could set it up as soon as you can," ended Felix. He said goodbye and the call was over.

She thought it would be easy to get information that could help Olivia. She'd thought wrong. Maybe getting Felix involved had not been such a good idea. Besides, she hadn't exactly agreed to his tit-for-tat arrangement. Although she hadn't disagreed, which meant she was stuck with it.

* * *

Chase read through Harley's will in the office of Harley's personal attorney that morning. Chase knew when Harley had married Olivia there was a prenup, of course, but Harley had been very generous to her in his will. Ridiculously generous. When Harley died, as his wife Olivia was to receive the house in Milton, as well as $75 million. Which Chase thought was crazy. Of course, Atherton Global had been left to Chase in its entirety, but it galled him that Olivia's inheritance was so substantial. They'd only been married for a year for God's sake, but there was nothing Chase could do about it. Olivia definitely had wrapped Harley around her little finger, and now that he was dead she would end up with a fortune.

Unless she was found guilty of murder.

He was well aware in that case she would inherit nothing, not a dime. Or the house either. Convicted criminals are prohibited from receiving any benefit from their crime, and the thought of Olivia tried, convicted, and in prison was a good one. Having her penniless and behind bars, was even better. A lot better. In fact, it was perfect.

* * *

Madeline called Olivia the next day, basically just to make sure she hadn't been arrested and was now in jail. Madeline had to follow up, it was her responsibility now. Olivia had said she was the only one looking out for her.

"I'm just checking in, to see how you are doing?" she asked when Olivia answered. So, she wasn't in jail, because one of the first things the police do when a suspect is booked is to take away their cell phone. At least that's what the cops did on TV.

"It's so good to hear from you, Madeline. I'm glad Harley's funeral is behind me now because it was incredibly sad, heartbreaking really. I don't know how I managed to get through it. About twenty-five of his relatives flew in from Pennsylvania. I'd met a couple of them at the wedding, but I was surprised so many of them came for his funeral. Three of them even politely hinted about the will, but I ignored their questions."

"What an awful day," said Madeline. "Have you heard anything more from the police about the investigation?"

"I have, and it's bad, in fact, I am very nervous now. Chase apparently told the police that Harley and I had been in a big argument on the patio right before he was shot. I can hardly believe it! It isn't true of course. I never saw Chase on the patio that day, I didn't even know he was at our place until the police arrived. I have absolutely no idea why he would say we were arguing on the patio. I did tell Harley how much I loved the emerald necklace, and I don't know, maybe I was too emphatic or something, and Chase misunderstood my tone."

"Harley and I have never argued about anything. Ever." Olivia sighed. "Anyway, when the police told me what Chase said, I knew I should have a lawyer, so I made some calls, and now I have a lawyer, a criminal lawyer, supposedly the best in Boston, with years of experience. With what I'm paying him he should be able to retire when it's over for God's sake. Anyway, never mind about that. If the police want to talk to me again, I'll have him with me."

"That is great news," said Madeline. "I'm relieved you have a lawyer and it sounds like he's a good one."

"He is very smart; two books have been written about cases he's won. Anyway, I told him about Chase and his statement to the police about me and Harley, and he was very clear that I am not to speak with Chase again, under any circumstances without him present." There was a silence, and

82

then Olivia said, "My lawyer is calling me now on the other line. I have to go." and she disconnected.

Madeline sighed. Why would Chase throw Olivia under the bus? When Chase came to the store with Edgar, she could tell he didn't much care for Olivia. But why would he make up something so damning? He'd have to have been aware of the conclusion the police would draw, so he had done it on purpose. Why?

But more to the point, Olivia had an experienced lawyer now who would be totally focused on her interests, which for Madeline meant she didn't need to feel responsible anymore. Besides, Olivia's lawyer could help her a lot more than she ever could. The expensive lawyer could figure out what to do next.

Although Madeline still felt bad, because she knew she hadn't tried all that hard to help Olivia. She had barely lifted a finger, all she'd done was call Felix. Which had proved to be a waste of time. Not only that, but now she had to worry about getting Olivia to agree to meet with Felix, which had a 'when pig's fly' feeling written all over it.

* * *

Madeline woke up immediately when her phone rang just after midnight and she looked at the caller ID. It was Abby.

Madeline began with, "Something's wrong. What's happened?"

"It's my mother, she's in surgery right now in Chicago. She went into cardiogenic shock, which is like heart failure, but more serious, and usually happens to people who've already had a heart attack. I'm in a cab on my way to the airport. They are taking her into surgery now. I talked to the surgeon and he said it's touch and go."

"Oh, dear. I'm sorry to hear that. Send me a text as soon as she's out of surgery? I'll call Martin first thing in the morning and have him come in."

"You will? Good, very good, thank you. I'm glad."

At least one of them was glad.

Still, if having Martin come in would relieve some of the stress for Abby, she was happy to do it. Well, not exactly happy, but she'd manage.

* * *

Martin showed up at precisely 9:00 the next morning, and it was the same everything; slicked-back hair, black patent leather shoes, even the blue glasses, and of course his umbrella in a blue nylon sheath tucked under his arm. Except today his suit was a dark olive green.

"Any update from Abby?" he asked when he walked in.

"Thank you for coming in on such short notice. I haven't heard anything since we talked last night."

"No news is good news. After we hung up, I googled cardiogenic shock. It has a fifty percent survival rate."

"Thanks for that cheery information," said Madeline, and then went back to an online jewelry auction on her computer.

At 9:15 Donia walked in the door, and Martin stared disapprovingly at her dull gray slacks and bulky parka. Madeline smiled and walked up to her. "I am so sorry," she said to Donia, "But I don't have a thing in bullet-proof diamond bracelets today. Maybe later in the week?"

Martin stared at Madeline, and after five seconds, he laughed.

Donia grinned. "I was in the area and I thought I'd drop by. Plus, I do have some info."

"Let's go to the office," said Madeline, and they walked to the back.

"Who's the guy with the blue glasses?"

"He's our backup, because Abby had to fly back to Chicago. Her mother had emergency surgery last night and they inserted an intra-aortic pump, whatever that is. Abby doesn't know when she'll be back."

"I'm sorry to hear that. I hope all goes well for her. Anyway, this is just something I heard, so it's not official, it's only forensics gossip. And I want to help you because someday maybe you'll help me. With a name. From that old case, you know. All I need is a name."

"Oh that. Sorry, but no."

Donia shrugged. "Someday you'll tell me."

Madeline shook her head, then said, "Whatever. Donia, you'll be glad to know that I have ended my 'unofficial interest' in Harley Atherton's murder. I did some checking around on something, but it was a dead end. I did try though. Anyway, the wife has a criminal lawyer now, so she doesn't need my help anymore."

"Well, that is good news. You won't want to hear my forensic information then."

"Like what? Not that I'm curious." A pause, and then, "Alright, I am curious. A little bit curious."

"I figured you would be. Anyway, there is a procedure, called 'Muzzle to Distance Targeting,'" used for the reconstruction of a shooting. It's a microscopic examination of a shooting victim's clothing to determine how far away the victim was from the muzzle of the gun. Which can be helpful, except in Harley's case."

"Why not?"

"Because after he was shot his body was moved—dragged actually on the patio. Not far it would seem, but enough so the microscopic evidence from the entrance wound on his back and on his shirt was contaminated with gravel and dirt. So, it's a waste of time. I don't know why the body was moved. It shouldn't have happened, especially not at a murder scene."

"Well, I know why. I helped Olivia roll Harley on his back—so she could perform CPR," said Madeline. "And then she pulled his body down a bit from a grassy incline, so that he would be lying flat on the tiles on the patio, so that's where the gravel and dirt would have come from."

"That explains the contamination then. Interesting, so the rest shouldn't matter to you."

"What do you mean, 'the rest'? I'd like to know what else you have, because why not?

"Well, it's not much, but it does mean that the shooter could have been standing very close to Harley, or the shooter could have been standing ten or even twenty feet away. Which neither hurts nor helps Olivia, it just makes everything …unclear. But you don't care since you're not involved."

"That's true. Except for the fact that if Olivia is charged and tried, I'll be called as an 'Eyewitness for the Prosecution', I think it's called."

"You need to stop watching cop shows, it's warping you. Anyway, I wanted to tell you what I heard. I said I'd let you know if I heard anything that I wouldn't feel uncomfortable repeating."

"Thank you, Donia, I do appreciate the update."

They walked to the front of the store.

"Nice place you've got here," said Donia. "Swank," She looked around, "and Boston symphony season posters no less. You really have gone 'uptown' haven't you?"

Madeline sighed, "I'm afraid so. Let's have dinner soon though. Catch up."

"Yes, let's. And I am seriously glad to know that you're no longer involved in another murder investigation."

"Now that Olivia, the wife, has hired a 'dragon-slayer' of a lawyer, I am off the hook, so to speak," said Madeline. "I am still a witness though, but I am definitely not checking into a crime of murder. Although this time, I would have almost been licensed to have a gun. Which possibly might have come in handy, but now I'll never know. Sort of too bad, isn't it?"

"Not really. I hope this murder case turns out better for you than that last one with the widow that you were in up to your neck."

Madeline laughed as Donia walked out the door. And then she stopped laughing since it wasn't all that funny. She was lucky she hadn't been killed.

Chapter Seven

Driving to Coda Gems that morning she decided that Martin wasn't all that bad. Until she heard Martin tell their first customer of the day, a woman from Marblehead, "You have the most beautiful platinum fox coat I have ever seen in my life."

First of all, the coat wasn't fox, it was lynx; second, lynx is an endangered species; and third, the coat wasn't beautiful, it was ugly.

The rest of the morning wasn't much better. Madeline spent half an hour talking to a deeply tanned customer, a sailor no doubt, about their Sea Dweller Rolex watch with a $10,000 price tag. The man was very interested and said he'd buy it. But then, after he took out his credit card, he looked at the watch again, changed his mind, and left.

"I knew he wasn't going to buy," said Martin after the man had walked out the door.

"And how did you know that?" said Madeline, annoyed.

"I'm psychic," he said with a patronizing smile and walked away.

Madeline stared after him. She knew she would end up with at least one, possibly two personality disorders if she had to work with Martin for more than a couple of days.

* * *

Olivia strolled into the store in the afternoon, in dark gray cashmere slacks and blazer, and headed straight to the glass case with their emerald collection.

"Hi, Madeline. I've been thinking about getting a pair of emerald earrings, teardrop ones, to match my beautiful necklace. About four carats would be good, each. I don't think I saw any like that when I was here before, but I thought I'd double-check and see if anything new had come in."

The thought fleetingly flashed in Madeline's mind; is this the way a new widow acts? But she dismissed it. She said as she walked up to Olivia, "The only emerald earrings we have are square-shaped, two carats each."

"I just told you I'm interested in tear-drop, with four carats of emeralds. Each."

That stopped Madeline cold, "Understood." It looked like Olivia was back to her old, supercilious self. Madeline forced a smile, "I'll get in touch with my dealer and see if there were teardrop earrings fabricated to match your necklace, and if there weren't, what he can find in teardrop, four carats, each. What is your price range?"

"Good, and of course I'll want them with platinum settings, so they'll match my necklace. I think somewhere around thirty or thirty-five thousand would be good."

Madeline glanced at Martin whose eyes had opened wide at her $35,000 limit.

"Fine," said Madeline. "I'll see what my gem dealer can find. Do you have any photos of what you're looking for?"

"No, unfortunately, my mother's jewelry and any photos were destroyed years ago," said Olivia with a bleak laugh, "along with everything else."

Another thing Madeline had learned about the very rich is that they didn't like a lot of questions. If they wanted you to know something, they'd tell you.

Martin began, "So what happened…"

Madeline interrupted, saying to Olivia as she grabbed a pad of paper and a pencil and handed it to her, "Can you give me a rough sketch of what you're looking for? That will be helpful."

Olivia set down her purse and expertly drew a sketch of a woman. Two-inch-long dangling earrings were set with big teardrop emeralds. "That's as near as I can remember." She handed the page to Madeline.

"Great. I'll get started right away. When do you want them?"

"As soon as possible," said Olivia, and picked up her purse. "By the way, do you know where Penelope is? No one at the office can find her. Which is annoying. She is on the payroll after all, and I need her."

"I have no idea where she is. At Harley's wake, Penelope did say she was taking some time off."

"Yes, she mentioned that to me as well, and I told her not to take time off now. This is so annoying, I have things for her to do. It would be helpful if you ask your police friend to look for her."

"Well, my friend is not a cop now, and she was in Homicide, not Missing Persons."

Olivia shrugged. "Well, if she can't do it, then you can at least look, if you don't mind." She took out a pen and scrawled a phone number and an address on a piece of paper and handed it to Madeline.

"Let me know what you find out." She turned to leave.

Martin stared after her. She didn't like it that Olivia was sending her on errands, but she could hardly say no. The woman was interested in buying a $35,000 pair of earrings from Coda Gems after all, which would make Abby happy. And her too of course.

Still, she didn't like it. At least Madeline no longer felt responsible for Olivia. She was now just a customer, a high-maintenance one with a well-developed sense of superiority and a lot of money. Like most of their customers.

* * *

Madeline tried calling Penelope several times that day, but no answer, just a recording that said her mailbox was full. After work, she drove to Penelope's building on Linnaean St. in Cambridge, buzzed her third-floor unit and Penelope's voice crackled through, "Who is it?"

"It's Madeline Lane, from Coda Gems." After she was buzzed in, she stepped into the creaky elevator and hit the button for the third floor. When the doors opened Penelope, in brown sweatpants and a sweater was waiting for her in the hallway.

"Hi, Madeline, come with me." Penelope led her down the hall and around a corner to her apartment.

"Olivia was concerned when she couldn't reach you," said Madeline as Penelope opened her door.

They walked into a small but beautiful apartment with hardwood floors and a black granite fireplace. The upholstered furniture in the living room was a delicate shade of pink.

"My phone is on the fritz," said Penelope, "I'm getting it fixed tomorrow."

Madeline said no to a drink and they sat in the living room, which overlooked a courtyard of bare trees and empty fire pits.

"What does Olivia want?" said Penelope.

"I have no idea. She asked me to find you, and now I have."

"Do you do everything Olivia wants?"

Madeline laughed. "She's a good customer."

"Well, so am I, I bought the Patek, remember?"

"True, you did buy a great watch. Thank you. It didn't take you long to make up your mind about it."

"I'd just come from a funeral that day," she said. "It was for an old friend, Wallace, who worked at Atherton Global years ago. I guess I needed a little pick me up after the service was over. It was sad, but then all funerals are sad. Nobody has a good time at a funeral, do they? I cried before, during, and after. I was a regular waterworks during his service, all those memories, you know?"

"I am sorry."

Madeline had been right, Penelope had known Wallace, and it seemed she'd known him fairly well. But that interesting information was no longer relevant, given that Madeline had dropped her 'unofficial interest' in finding a connection between Wallace and Harley's deaths.

Penelope continued, "Wallace called me out of the blue a couple of days before he died, and said he wanted to get together for drinks, something about seeing a recent photo in the newspaper of a person he thought died years ago. Sounds creepy doesn't it?" She sighed, "He was just like me you know, he had a photographic memory, except his was better. Anyway, we used to talk about well, we talked about everything back in the old days. We were supposed to meet for lunch, but that didn't happen. Turns out I ended up going to his funeral instead." Penelope sighed, and when tears slid down her cheeks she brushed them away. "It would have been so good to see him again. I talked to his wife Lucy at the service, who is not quite 'all there if you know what I mean. She doesn't really understand that Wallace is dead. It's very sad."

Madeline leaned forward in her chair. "What was Wallace like? I've heard people mention his name before, but I know nothing about him. It seems he was an interesting guy."

"He was an accountant," said Penelope, and laughed, "but he did have a wicked sense of humor. He even made fun of Harley, in front of him if you can believe it, but Harley was fond of him. And then one day years ago, Wallace up and quit, just like that. He was in Harley's office for an hour and I could hear them yelling at each other, something that Harley had ordered to be done and... There were things that happened then that I was not to know about. But I did." Penelope stopped, "I shouldn't be telling you this. I am not a gossip."

"But Penelope, that's not gossip, what you are talking about are facts," insisted Madeline, who didn't want her to stop. "And facts are not gossip, facts are information. I am curious though, something happened between Harley and Wallace?"

Penelope looked at her out of the corner of her eye, and repeated, "I am not a gossip, I'm just not." She shook her head firmly and settled back in her chair, "I wonder what Olivia needs?"

"Like I said, I have no idea."

Penelope gave a big sigh.

"What's the matter?" asked Madeline.

"Nothing really, it's just that...oh, it's nothing I'm sure. Anyway, I'll call Olivia later. She can be hard as nails you know. She is the most determined woman I've ever known."

Penelope then talked about Harley for ten long minutes, and Madeline listened, not wanting to interrupt. According to Penelope, Harley was the most extraordinary man in the world. "He was such a kind boss, really. Although he wasn't the most perceptive man in the world. You would have thought he would be, but he wasn't. Stubborn as a mule actually. He believed what he wanted to believe, and that was that. But he was a good man, and he did love the military life. I always thought he would have looked splendid in a general's uniform."

She glanced at her watch, the Patek. "Oh dear, I'm late. Sorry but I have to call my mother right now. She lives in Hull and I call her every night before she goes to bed."

Madeline stood up. "Penelope, I'm glad I found you for Olivia. Please do give her a call tonight though. She was worried about you."

"Was she really?" said Penelope. "That's unusual." She walked Madeline to the door and said, "You're in an interesting business, selling expensive jewelry, and watches. You must meet all kinds of different people."

"I certainly do."

"Then you must know," she said with a small smile as they stood in the doorway, "that people might not always be what they seem. She, I mean they, they might be a different person altogether." Penelope shook her head. "Well, anyway, it was good of you to come by." Penelope glanced at an oversized clock on the living room wall. "I'll call Olivia right after I talk to Mother. There must be something she wants me to do."

Madeline said good night and walked to the elevator. She should never have agreed to look for Penelope. She didn't run personal errands for customers.

Their legs weren't broken, they could run their own errands.

Chapter Eight

C hase was not in a good mood the next morning at the Atherton Global offices. He had been absolutely positive that Olivia would have been arrested by now. She should have been arrested immediately after Harley had been shot, but that hadn't happened. When he'd asked the detective in charge about it, he'd been told the case wasn't necessarily a cut-and-dried domestic one.

"We have to look at possible external motives," was all Detective Vanasse would say, "given Mr. Atherton's military business."

The last thing Chase wanted was to have state police detectives scrutinizing their client records, which meant the sooner Olivia was charged with his murder the better.

When Edgar showed up at Chase's door and said, "Got a minute?" Chase motioned him in.

"I do."

The problem with Edgar, or rather one of the problems with Edgar, was that he thought he was smarter than Chase. He wasn't. Chase was brilliant, and he knew it. On the other hand, Edgar was the best operations man in the organization, and hands-down, the best marksman, and Chase was about the worst. Chase just didn't have that much interest in putting bullet holes in silhouettes. He thought it was boring and noisy.

Chase looked at the stack of paperwork Penelope had left on his desk. Harley had hardly given a thought to his own mortality; he had been too busy running Atherton Global. At least there was a will, a fifty-page will, but Harley hadn't gotten around to developing a succession plan for the company or spend time grooming Chase to be in charge. And now all of a sudden, he was the new CEO running a big company with offices in five countries. Chase knew he could handle it, but unfortunately, he needed Edgar, since he knew more about the day-to-day operation of the company than anyone except Harley.

Edgar sat down in a chair across from Chase, staring at him with his usual steely gaze. "I need to take some time off. It's been a while since I've taken any time, and I need a couple of weeks, or so."

Chase noted that Edgar wasn't asking him, he was telling him. The two men hadn't spoken since Harley's burial service at the cemetery. As they watched Harley's casket lowered into the ground, Edgar had told Chase to send him Wallace's files that he'd taken home, and Chase said he couldn't, because he'd already shredded them.

He hadn't. The files were in a file drawer in his home office, and Chase meant to go through them when he had time.

Chase looked at Edgar as he sat across from him in his office and said, "It would be better if you could wait two or three months to take time off. There are five annual contracts coming up for renewal, and one of them is the UAE's, and I've got to replace the regional manager in the Ukraine, as well as the one in Kenya. It would be good if you could wait."

"No, I need the time off now, for personal reasons. I talked to Harold Ritscher this morning, and he has the bandwidth to help you. He is the best there is, and he can give you advice if you need it. Like I said, I have to take time off."

Harold was relatively new to Atherton Global, a man who had commanded nine hostage rescue teams in his Delta Force career before he retired from the Army. The man was basically a 'celebrity hire' in the private military contractor world. Harley had brought him into Atherton Global because he knew the Pentagon, their biggest client, would like it.

They did.

Chase had to be careful since he was now Edgar's boss, a situation he guessed Edgar hated. Chase knew he would have to fire him, but he'd do it only when the time was right.

"What is it that you need to do? Maybe we can help," said Chase. Careful not to phrase it as, "Maybe I can help."

Edgar looked at Chase and hesitated before he said, his eyes glinting, "I need to go to Paris and find out why Harley dropped everything and flew there last week. What was so all-fire important, and who did he meet with? That's what I want to find out."

Chase wanted to know too. "That's a good idea. I guess we can manage without you for a week but go as an Atherton Global employee so all your expenses will be covered. I'll want to be updated while you're there of course."

Edgar stood up, "Thanks. Two weeks will do. I'll leave in a couple of days," and he left.

Chase stared after him. He'd have fired him on the spot, but he needed Edgar. For now.

Penelope walked in with his mail in a creaky leather Army Air Corp. aviator bag, which had been Chase's grandfather's, from World War II. Harley had liked little touches like that, Chase not so much. He told Penelope that Edgar would be taking a week off and asked her to set up a two-hour meeting with him and Harold to bring him up to speed on Edgar's training schedules. She nodded and left.

Chase leaned back in his chair. Yes, he quite liked being the boss, even under such horrible circumstances. He had big plans to re-organize Atherton Global, and he was looking forward to it. First, he needed to hire artificial intelligence, robotics, and thinking machine experts and move the company into the twenty-first century. His long-term plan though, which he'd developed right after he got his MBA, was for Atherton Global to become a long-term military partner with the US government, and the EU as well. They had the potential to become the Goldman Sachs of private military contractors—they could be world-class advisors. The ways of waging war were changing, and Chase wanted Atherton Global to be the leader. He'd talked to Harley a number of times about shifting their focus and become a 'strategic engine' for their clients instead of their 'iron fist.' None of those conversations with Harley had gone well, and Harley's response had always been the same, "No," ending with, "over my dead body."

Which as it was turning out, had been more or less prophetic.

Still, Harley's murder was hanging over Atherton Global like a thunder cloud, and the case needed to be solved as soon as possible. He thought about Madeline Lane, who seemed to be Olivia's best friend now. He couldn't figure out what Madeline was up to, but she was definitely up to something. She was either a loose end or a loose cannon.

He'd have to figure out a way to get her alone and have a bit of a chat. He needed to find out which one she was, and then deal with that.

* * *

Early the next morning Sam emailed Madeline two photos of emerald earrings for Olivia, along with their GIA appraisals. The earrings in the first photo had a total of seven carats of emeralds with platinum settings that were not an exact match with the platinum chain in Olivia's necklace, but very close. The earrings in the second photo, with a total of eight carats, were a better match, but the color of the stones was not as intense of a green as the large emerald in Olivia's necklace. Although it was hard to be sure since it was only a photo. She called Sam.

"Thanks for the photos, but can you have both sets of earrings sent to me overnight?"

"Sure thing. I don't know who your customer is, but I love him."

"Me too. Although it's a 'her'. And thanks for finding them so quickly."

"You know Madeline since you and Abby have moved to your new location, the quality of your customers has definitely improved."

"You mean because they have more money?"

"Yes."

"They do indeed." She said goodbye and disconnected.

* * *

Madeline called Olivia right away. "Hey, Olivia, it's Madeline. I'll have two sets of emerald earrings here for you to look at tomorrow. You can stop by anytime and let me know what you think."

"So soon? That's great, Madeline, I'm very impressed. What time should I be there?"

"Let's say one o'clock?"

"Perfect. See you then!"

Martin had overheard the call and commented, "I hope Olivia likes the earrings."

"She will. One of the sets is perfect, and I'm pretty sure she'll love it."

"Her husband was just murdered in Milton, wasn't he?"

Madeline hadn't mentioned that to Martin. She said, "Yes, he was murdered. The state police are investigating."

"Any suspects?"

"It's still early in the investigation, and no, they don't have any *real* suspects."

Which she said so emphatically that Martin looked up, a ruby bracelet in his hand. "No suspects? None? Really, none? I always suspect the spouse first. Always. It's a pretty safe bet, in my opinion, so I'm going with the wife. Guilty as charged."

The man was impossible. Madeline took a deep breath, and said, "Well Martin, that just might be because you're an idiot."

Martin shrugged and continued re-arranging their ruby jewelry in the glass case furthest from the door. Which she had just carefully arranged when she'd come in that morning, putting a bracelet that she'd just bought the week before, a showstopper with eleven carats of rubies, front and center. But now Martin had positioned it off to the side, along with three heavily set ruby rings. An interesting design, but she didn't like it.

She'd change the display after Martin went home. She didn't want to offend him twice on the same day.

Abby needed to come back to Boston sooner rather than later.

* * *

Olivia walked into the store at precisely 1:00 the next day. Madeline led her to the office, placed a vanity mirror in front of her, and brought out the two sets of emerald earrings. Olivia was wearing the emerald necklace, the pendant tucked under her scarf, which was a good idea. No sense in flaunting fourteen carats of AAA-rated emeralds to the general public. Olivia pulled off her scarf, picked up the emerald earrings, attached them to her ear lobes, and smiled at her reflection in the mirror. They were a perfect match with her necklace. She watched herself in the mirror as she turned her head, the emeralds glowing under the overhead lights.

"These are great," Olivia said. "Absolutely great. Exactly what I wanted. How much?" She didn't bother to even pick up the second set of earrings.

"Thirty-three thousand, five hundred."

"Perfect, I'll take them." She opened her purse and took out a black American Express card. "No need to put them in a box, I want to wear them."

"They are fabulous, especially with your necklace."

"They are indeed." Olivia squeezed Madeline's hand, "Just what I need right now."

"Yes, well, I'm very happy you like them."

The two women walked out to the front, and because of the amount, Madeline called American Express with the charge and was transferred to the head of customer service.

While Madeline waited for the head of AmEx customer service to pick up, Olivia said, "I'm staying at the Four Seasons. I'm just not sure what I will do next, or where I want to live. My whole life is on hold for now." She hesitated before she said, "To make matters even worse, I think I am being followed."

Madeline's head jerked up. "Followed?"

"Yes."

"By the police?"

"I assume so."

"You can tell that someone is following you?"

"Yes, I know when I am being followed. I also know how to shake a tail, so it's not the end of the world."

Madeline just stared at Olivia, whose brown eyes were grim. Where, and why had Olivia learned that? Then AmEx came back on the line, Madeline handed the phone to Olivia, and after three quick questions, the charge was approved.

"Followed? I don't know what to say," commented Madeline as she rang up the sale.

Olivia shrugged. "I told my lawyer two days ago and he said he'd check into that with the police, but he hasn't gotten back to me. I just don't know what is going on."

"He should have gotten back to you immediately."

"I thought so too."

"Do you want me to come back with you to the hotel? Martin can handle any customers that—"

"No, absolutely not. I'm sorry, I shouldn't have mentioned it. I'll be fine, just fine."

Olivia looked in the mirror at her earrings one last time, signed the receipt, said "Goodbye," and walked out the door, Madeline staring after her. Even though Olivia supposedly had a top-notch lawyer, he didn't seem to be of much use.

She called Olivia an hour later. "I'm just checking, to be sure you're alright and you got back to your hotel."

Olivia sighed, "Yes, I'm in my hotel room. Don't worry about me though, I'll be fine. Just fine."

* * *

Still, Madeline was alarmed that Olivia was being followed and her lawyer didn't seem to be concerned. What good was he? She couldn't walk away from looking out for Olivia just yet. She called Felix because maybe he would have a good idea. After all, he had gotten in touch with one of his precious sources with the New Hampshire State Police to get information on the shooting of the Wallace guy for her. Even if the quid pro quo was that she had to set up a meeting with Olivia for him.

Felix didn't pick up, so she left a message so he'd know she hadn't forgotten, "Still waiting to hear about a meeting with Olivia, but I do have a question.

Let me know when we can connect."

Five minutes later he shot a text, "Let's meet? That new place, where Les Zygomates used to be, near South Station."

Madeline looked around, there were no customers in the store, and Martin was talking on his phone, staring at a Boston Symphony poster from 1933. So, she could leave. She replied to Felix, "I'll be there in ten minutes."

She grabbed a cab, and ten minutes later walked into the new wine bar, its walls covered with framed posters from the 1930s and 1940s. At least that hadn't changed. Felix was sitting in the back, his eyes on the door, just like in the old days. Except today he looked tired, and he hadn't shaved that morning. As she walked up, he ran his fingers through his hair, which was thinning. She hadn't noticed that before.

She pulled out a chair and ordered a cup of cappuccino from the waiter.

"I don't know why you drink that," he said. "It's not really coffee. It's more like a bonbon for God's sake."

Madeline shrugged. "Like I said in my message, I'm just waiting for a good time to set up a meeting for you with Olivia. She's still in shock."

"Thanks," said Felix. "I definitely do want to talk to her. When do you think would be a good time?"

Madeline wanted to say, "Never," which was not a good idea, so instead, she said, "I'm working on it, and I'll let you know. By the way, Olivia thinks the police are following her."

Felix's eyebrows shot up. "Madeline, these days the police don't usually have the staff or the time to put people under surveillance. If Olivia is indeed being followed, it's probably not by the police. She's sure she's being followed?"

"That's what she said."

"And she thinks it's the police?"

Madeline nodded.

"It probably isn't, but who knows?" said Felix. "Maybe it is. Anyway, I'd like to talk to her before she's arrested, charged, tried, and sent to prison. It can be hard to talk to a convicted murderer once they're in the slammer."

When it came to getting a story, Felix could be coldblooded.

"I'm just waiting for the right time."

Felix's cell phone rang, and he didn't even look at the caller ID. This time he really was paying attention to her.

"Good, because I do want to talk to her. Just so you know, I did a little more digging into your dead guy, Harley," said Felix. "Like I told you, his company was involved in some nasty things years ago. He didn't mind getting drawn into civil wars, it was how he made his living back then. Harley's father, Daniel, who founded Atherton Global, was, a bloody SOB, and I mean that literally. When Harley worked for his father, the International Criminal Court, which everybody just calls the ICC, investigated both of them for war crimes in North Africa, in Algeria as I recall. By the way, the ICC is the only international organization that can indict and try individuals for war crimes, the UN can't. Anyway, a small town, El-Traynor, at least I think that was the name, was bombed. Since it was not a military target it was a huge story at the time, because a couple thousand civilians died. That's what Harley and his father were investigated for, but no surprise, nothing came of it."

"When was that?"

"In the early part of the century. This one," he added with a smile. "I'm very interested in the guy now, so tell me more about him."

For the next ten minutes, Madeline told him everything she knew about Harley.

She ended by saying, "Like I said, I'll work on setting up a time for you to talk to Olivia soon."

"Could you sound a bit more positive?"

"How about I will set it up as soon as she feels up to it?"

His cell phone rang again. But this time, after checking the caller ID, he took the call, whispering to Madeline, "I have to take this. Let me know as soon as possible when I can talk to Olivia. And thanks."

She whispered a goodbye, dropped a twenty-dollar bill on the table, and left. She was even more worried about Olivia now that she knew it probably wasn't the police who were following her. It would have been better if it had been the cops, because if it wasn't the police, it could only be Atherton Global, which wasn't good. To make matters worse, she was definitely and firmly on the hook to get Olivia to talk to Felix, which wouldn't be easy. Now that Madeline thought about it, the mere suggestion of Felix interviewing Olivia for his series on Gun Deaths in New England would give her new lawyer a heart attack. Which maybe he deserved.

She'd just have to figure a way out of this, but she was almost done. Almost. For all Madeline knew the police might even be closing in on charging a real suspect with Harley's murder. It could happen any day.

* * *

Madeline called Abby every night while she was in Chicago, telling her about the day's sales, the customers who'd come in, and any new pieces of jewelry she thought they should buy. Abby tracked their sales on a daily basis with her computer, so Madeline and Abby's daily conversations weren't all that different than usual, except it was now by phone, text, email, or Zoom, which was not the same, and Madeline was lonely. She had bought a new pair of lavender cowboy boots two days before and had worn them to the store the next day. If Abby had been there, she would have rolled her eyes when Madeline walked in. Madeline never thought she'd miss that, but she did. Martin, on the other hand, had looked her up and down when he'd come in and said, "You know, you dress like you are on your way to a square dance, pretty much every day." Which was almost funny.

She missed Abby's cool competence, her quick assessments, and, well, even her conservative predictability.

"So how has Martin been?" Abby asked Madeline that night when they talked.

"Martin? Sorry, but I killed him this morning. I tried to control myself, but I was sadly not successful."

"Seriously Madeline, how has it been going between the two of you?"

"It's been fine. I basically don't pay any attention to him. It's alright I guess."

"He did sell a $10,000 Gurhan bracelet two days ago. And an $11,000 ruby ring yesterday plus two Tiffany bracelets, which was excellent."

"When will you be back again?"

"In seven days."

"I thought it was six."

"No, seven."

"And your mother is doing well?"

"Yes, thanks. Her doctors are impressed with her quick recovery, and the long-term prognosis is good, well sort of good. She and my dad play cribbage constantly, and I am learning canasta, so life is splendid." Abby hated to play cards.

Madeline said, "Liz Schuvart has just launched a new collection of ruby jewelry. Have you been on her website yet? I sent you a list yesterday of the pieces I want to buy. A purchase order for ninety thousand dollars will cover it. We'll get the pieces in a month if the order is placed tomorrow."

"I did check it out, and her ruby jewelry is great, and minimalist designs are selling these days, so I'll email her a purchase order tomorrow. And congrats again on selling Harley's wife the emerald earrings. I have to say, that was a big, impressive sale. You did very well."

"Thank you. She can be demanding, and rude, but I must be getting used to her."

"Well, that's good news."

Abby then brought up an Art Deco jewelry auction in New York coming up that Madeline had talked for a month about going to, but then had changed her mind, three times. Which was beginning to irritate Abby.

"Madeline, I think you should definitely go to the auction in New York. I've taken a look at the link you sent, and yes, you should definitely go. It would be good to have a new collection of Art Deco, and especially anything Bakelite."

"I suppose I really should." Madeline hesitated, "Martin should be fine running the store for one day. I mean, what could possibly go wrong?"

"Don't be ridiculous, he's been there by himself a million times. You should go, we need some new pieces in the store."

"You're right, so fine, I'll definitely go."

"Yes, that would be good."

Abby didn't ask about Harley's murder investigation and Madeline was not about to bring it up. She hadn't told Abby yet that Olivia was a suspect, and likely the prime one in the investigation. Much less that Madeline had been sort of involved in investigating the murder. That was something that Abby just didn't need to know.

The two partners wished each other a good night and hung up.

Chapter Nine

The next morning the headline in *The Boston Globe* was big, and bold. Even then Madeline had to read it twice because she couldn't believe it: *Wife in Milton Arrested in Husband's Murder.* Madeline's heart stopped. She quickly read the short article. Olivia had been arrested and was now in jail at the state police barracks in Milton. At least the charge was not Murder One but second-degree murder, which is still murder, the only difference between the two is the state police believed Olivia had shot and killed Harley, but without premeditation. Madeline threw down the paper and called Donia.

"My friend Olivia has been arrested," began Madeline. "Murder in the second degree."

"Yes, I know, and I am sorry. I heard it on the radio this morning on my way to work."

"This is terrible, absolutely terrible. A nightmare. What will happen now?"

"Well, the police don't like having arrested murder suspects released on bail, but there will be a bail hearing. And if she has no prior record and can come up with a lot of money, I'm thinking a million or so, a really good lawyer can get her released. Otherwise, she'll stay in jail until the trial. I assume the police have no other suspects?"

Madeline sighed. "I don't think they do. Still, all they have is circumstantial evidence."

"You don't know what they have," Donia pointed out. "She does have a good lawyer, doesn't she?"

"Her lawyer is experienced, and I do know he's expensive, but I'm not actually sure how good he is. I can't believe she's been arrested! This is just unbelievable! From what I can tell, the state police aren't looking at other suspects, just Olivia, which is outrageous. Harley was in a dangerous business, and I'm sure he's made plenty of enemies over the years. The police need to know they have made a big mistake."

"Whatever you do, do not go see the state police and tell them they've made a mistake. They won't appreciate that. You'll just have to be patient."

"I have a couple of virtues, but patience, oddly enough, doesn't happen to be one of them."

"Well, it wouldn't hurt to work on that."

"I can't. I'm too busy."

"I'm sorry Madeline, but I need to go. I have to keep several billion dollars in art safe from bad guys with educated tastes." Donia hung up.

* * *

It seemed to Madeline that no one was doing anything to help Olivia. Well, her lawyer was most likely doing something, but if he was that good Olivia wouldn't have been charged with second-degree murder in the first place. And not only that, now that Olivia had been arrested, Madeline could no longer duck her responsibility, she had to actually do something significant to get the police to focus on someone else. Anyone else. All she needed to do was get the cops pointed in another direction, preferably the right one.

The only real lead she had was Wallace's files. She didn't know what exactly was in them, but it seemed to her it had to be bad. As a concerned citizen, Madeline could tell the police that she'd overheard Chase tell Edgar that he took home some old files from Wallace's time in Atherton Global's archives because…because he was afraid the police would find them? Well, he didn't say that, but it was implied. Edgar did tell Chase not to tell the police that he had them, which was a good indication that he believed there might be something in them he didn't want the police to see. But that wasn't the kind of information that would get the police to do anything besides raise their eyebrows.

But now that Olivia had been arrested, Madeline most definitely wanted the police to have a look at Chase's files. In a perfect world, they'd find something of interest and would start investigating real suspects right away and drop the murder charge against Olivia.

The problem was that Madeline had to first confirm the files were actually in Chase's possession. Which meant she had to go to his home. And then, she had to set about finding these files, and with any luck, snap some pictures with her cell phone, leave, and then convince the cops to swoop in and take the files as evidence before Chase or that damn Edgar could hide them. Or even worse, destroy them. Yes, that would be perfect.

She also knew it was a perfectly absurd plan, but she had to at least try. It never hurt to try.

Besides, doing nothing was not an option, and she didn't have any other leads.

The first part of her plan of course would be to somehow get inside Chase's home. Breaking in was out of the question; only a total idiot would try and break into the home of the owner of a private military contracting company.

She went over different ways to successfully get inside, and after only fifteen minutes came up with what she had to admit was a truly brilliant idea. In fact, it was genius. She went over it again, to make sure it wasn't harebrained, and it was a bit, but not entirely so. The point was that it was something she could absolutely, definitely pull off.

The second part, once she was inside Chase's home, was to actually find the files, which would be tricky. If she could just get her hands on them for even twenty seconds she could take cell phone pictures of ten or twenty pages for the police. Snooping was tacky, but at least it wasn't illegal.

Since Madeline was about to finagle her way into Chase's home, she should at least know something about the man, other than the fact that she didn't like him. She googled Chase Atherton, Boston, MA, and found him on LinkedIn. He was twenty-eight years old, went to boarding school in Miami, then to M.I.T. for a degree in electronics, and then on to their Sloan School of Management for an MBA. Chase was married and divorced, no kids, and was the Senior Vice President of Marketing at Atherton Global. Which wasn't much, but it was all the information she could find. Military contracting companies don't like publicity. Of any kind.

She hesitated to call Felix, but she called him anyway. Madeline knew she was pushing her luck with him, but she didn't have a choice. It was either Felix or nothing. If she was going to lie her way into Chase's home, she should at the very least know a bit more about him.

Felix returned her call seven hours later.

* * *

Madeline got right to the point when he answered, "Hey, Felix, thanks for getting back to me. Do you know anything about Harley's son, Chase Atherton? I searched on the internet, but all I could find was education and marital status, which wasn't particularly helpful. And I apologize for the bother, but I do need your advice."

"By the way, Madeline, I see that your friend Olivia just got arrested for second-degree murder."

"Yes, that. A miscarriage of justice if there ever was one. But what about Chase?"

"The answer is no. I don't know anything about him. Why are you asking? And don't tell me you're just curious."

"I'm trying to come up with information that can help Olivia, who, just so you know, might still be able to sit down and talk to you. Maybe. Possibly," She ended with, "Perhaps." She had to say that. She needed Felix. "Anyway," she said, "I'll let you know."

"Do."

"Back to Chase though. I am thinking he might have something in his background that could be of interest."

"Like what?"

Felix sighed, "Specifics would be helpful."

"Fine then. It would be good to know if he is a Level Three Sex Offender or something."

"I have no idea if he is, or not. Why do you want to know? Are you planning on dating him?"

"Cute. Anyway, I thought you'd know a thing or two about him, since you know everything, or know how to find out everything."

"Not quite," and he hung up.

Yes, Felix was annoyed which was too bad. For her.

* * *

Frustrated, Madeline checked her calendar. Chase could still be at Harley's place in Chatham. She should at least find out when he'd be back. She called Atherton Global and asked to speak to him, thinking the receptionist would tell her when he'd be returning. But to her surprise, she was transferred instead, and Chase picked up immediately. She wasn't expecting that.

"Hello, Madeline."

"Oh. Hi. Hi Chase. Do you have a minute?"

"Yes, I have a minute. How can I help you?"

She swallowed hard. The only thing she could do was plunge ahead. "Well, again my sympathies. Anyway, Harley was a good customer, and I would like to show my appreciation by...well, let me explain. I know that Harley had a collection of Patek watches, which I'm sure is pretty valuable."

"Yes, it is."

"I've dealt in the high-end watch category before, so I know a fair amount about Patek watches, and have bought and sold a number of them. Anyway, I thought it would be helpful for you if I appraised his Patek watch collection for you, at no charge. That way you'll have a sense of its current value, for insurance purposes. It would make me happy to do that for you."

"Oh, I hadn't thought about that. I'll have to check, but I think he had his watches appraised about ten years ago."

"Then it's time it was done again. How many are there in his collection?"

"Eleven."

"That's a good-size collection. It would probably be easier to do the appraisal at your place then, since—"

"That's an interesting idea, because I already have his watches in my safe here, at my home in Concord. I didn't want to leave them in his safe in Milton, what with the police and investigators tromping around outside, and in the house."

"Of course not," she said. "Well, think about it. The way I usually work is to do a very initial evaluation at the customer's home. I've found it's just easier that way because the watches won't need to be taken anywhere, so no insurance worries you know. I'd be happy to take a look at them. At your place."

She paused, giving him time to respond, and she realized she was holding her breath. Probably because pretty much everything she'd just told him she'd made up. On the spot. And she'd only ever sold one Patek before, to Penelope. Still, she did know a bit about the brand.

"Well, I guess that is a good idea," said Chase slowly. "You wouldn't mind then, coming to my home?"

"No, I wouldn't mind at all. It will take about an hour or two, and I'll bring my computer and get set up at a desk, in your home office would be good. Again, it would just be an initial appraisal. I'm sure Harley has paperwork for his watches, along with the old appraisals. I'll want to see those as well."

"Yes, he has a big file of paperwork, and I have that here too. I was going to take the watches and the old appraisals to the Bank of America and put them in my safe deposit box there next week."

"Then my timing is perfect. I can come to your place whenever is convenient for you. Just let me know."

"I'm opening my calendar now. I work from home on Fridays, so let's see, tomorrow about two o'clock would be good."

She didn't expect him to so readily agree, and certainly not for a meeting the next day, but she said, smoothly, "Let me see...well yes, as it turns out two can work for me as well."

Chase gave her his address, they exchanged cell phone numbers and he hung up.

She stared at her phone for a long minute. She was shocked that her brilliant idea had worked. To be honest, Madeline didn't think it would. She must be better at this than she thought.

However, while it was a brilliant way to get into Chase's home it didn't necessarily mean it was a good idea. There was a difference. Still, she wasn't about to ask for anyone's opinion. She knew they'd tell her it was a horrible, crazy-bad plan.

All Madeline wanted, now that it was set up, was to get it over with. At least she'd only have to wait a day. Besides, all she would really be doing was looking around, and if she was lucky, find some old files and take pictures. Or not.

At the very least she would have really tried to help Olivia this time, so doing something difficult would make her feel better. After all, Olivia was the only person who had actually ever saved her life.

* * *

The next day, at 1:55, Madeline drove down Chase's long, winding driveway, with towering pines on either side of the narrow, private road. Chase answered the doorbell in jeans and an M.I.T. sweatshirt, and led her through a dark hallway to his study in the back, with heavy, looming bookcases that held neat rows of leather-bound books, huge windows that looked out on a virtual forest of trees, and a big, old-fashioned mahogany desk in the middle. A Huntsman leather watch box sat at one end of the desk. At the other end was an ebony inbox of manila folders.

"Thank you for coming," said Chase. "I thought this would be a good place where you can spread out and work. I'll be in the dining room, down the hall, and around the corner. Let me know if you need anything," and he left.

She glanced around the study and spotted a security camera above the door aimed at his desk, and another camera on the opposite wall that was also aimed at his desk. Which meant her ingenious plan to find the files wouldn't work. It's hard to snoop through a home office with a camera filming your every move. Madeline sighed. Then she had an idea. She stood up and walked down the hall to the dining room. "Sorry Chase, but could I bother you for a glass of water?"

"Of course."

She went back to the desk and heard footsteps walking down the hall, away from the study. Good. She stood up, did a good imitation of a stumble, and with one hand knocked the black inbox of folders to the floor, and the files slid out and slipped under the desk. That worked out nicely. She bent down and out of sight of the security cameras, flipped through them. Just contracts that needed a signature. She stacked them together and had just set them back in the inbox when Chase walked in with a glass of water. At least she knew they weren't what she was looking for.

"Thank you, Chase," she said.

He set a glass of water on a coaster, his eyes sliding across the desk, stopping at the ebony inbox of contracts for several long seconds. He smiled, "Let me know if you need anything else," and he walked out, but not before his eyes rested on the inbox of files on his desk again.

She looked down at the four desk drawers. Maybe that's where Wallace's files were. But there was no way she could get into the drawers without the security camera filming her.

Well, she had tried to find the files from Wallace's time. To be honest, she hadn't really believed her plan would work. It had been sort of an idiotic idea to begin with, but she had to at least try. This time she had really tried hard to help Olivia, it just didn't happen to work out.

Madeline sighed and started on the Patek watch evaluations. After all, she did have to produce an appraisal for Chase.

She opened the glove-leather Huntsman watch box that alone had to have cost at least $5,000. She counted the gleaming Patek watches, neatly displayed in four rows, all of them with solid gold bands; Harley had clearly not been the alligator strap type. She picked up the first watch, a Nautilus 5711 Chronograph. No surprise, it had the usual hours, minutes, seconds, and date, as well as a calendar. And an icon for the phases of the moon which to her was overkill. Only werewolves and vampires needed to know the phases of the moon.

She took out her computer and clicked open the website, Chrono24.com, the leading marketplace in the world for high-end watches. The site carried listings of verified dealers who sold only the high-end of high-end watches, and in less than a minute she found the Patek Nautilus 5711 model, with a listed price of $159,800. Harley had expensive tastes. Deducting markup, the watch was probably worth about $120,000. She drew up a quick chart, and entered the watch model, and a description, as well as the information from Harley's earlier appraisal, and she took three pictures of the watch with her cell phone.

As she worked in Chase's study, she felt a sense of unease. She was in an isolated old house alone with Chase, a man on the bat-shit side of intense. Madeline worked quickly; she just wanted to get away. A little over two hours later there was only one watch left, a heavy, solid eighteen-carat gold watch, from Patek's pricey 'Grand Complications' line. She'd saved this one for last because it was the best as well as likely the most expensive. She'd recognized it right away, of course, it was the watch Harley had worn the first time he'd walked into Coda Gems. It was impressive, beautiful, and heavy. She held it in her hand and turned it over. Unlike the others though, this watch had a date and an inscription engraved on the back that she could barely make out.

She took out a jeweler's cloth and polished the front and the back of the watch, as well as the heavy gold bracelet. She spent several more minutes polishing the inscription of the back, which read: *February 8, 2002: You Got Us Out, Son! Love, Dad*

She went on the Chrono14.com website, and this particular watch in the Grand Complications line was listed for $400,000. It was an astonishing watch. She took front and back photos of the watch plus two close-ups of the inscription. No wonder Harley had worn it every day.

* * *

Madeline set the watches back in the watch case, picked it up, slid her laptop in her computer bag, and walked down the hall to the dining room. Chase had set himself up at a burnished oak dining table, his laptop open, a stack of files, and an almost empty glass of water beside him. He looked up and smiled. She eyed his stack of files, if only she could look through those for just a minute or two. She glanced around the walls and saw two security cameras, and then she noticed a small one in a corner of the ceiling pointing towards the windows. There were cameras everywhere in Chase's house. It was a waste of time to even think about cameras since she didn't see how she could possibly get Chase to walk out of the dining room so she could rifle through his papers.

"Well," she began, trying not to sound disappointed, "I have most of the information I need. I'll do some additional research and send you my appraisals in a couple of days."

"Sounds good and thank you again for coming out to my place." Chase flipped open the watch box and checked the neat rows.

"That big gold one," she nodded to the Grand Complications watch, "is stunning. It's one of the most beautiful watches I've ever seen."

"It is something, isn't it? I'll probably sell the other watches, but I'll never sell that one. It was Dad's favorite, and he wore it all the time. My grandfather gave it to him, a long time ago." Chase picked up the watch, and clicked the gold band around his wrist, admiring the watch. He looked at her. "It will be good to have a current appraisal of his collection. Are you sure I can't pay you for this?"

Madeline shook her head. "No, it's fine, I'm glad to do it."

"Great, but do you have a minute? I have a couple of questions." He nodded to a dining room chair.

"Sure." She sat down.

"I'm curious, just how well do you know Olivia?"

The question surprised her. "Why do you ask?"

"I don't know if you were aware, that she was arrested and charged with second-degree murder? I just heard she's out on bail already, which is unbelievable!" He looked at Madeline, his brown eyes dull, almost opaque, and he picked up his glass of water.

"Chase, I don't think Olivia murdered your father. I am positive it was someone else."

"Who else besides Olivia could have killed my father? Her mysterious 'man in brown'," and he laughed. "I have to confess, I am curious about something since you and Olivia are friends."

"Friends? Well, no, not exactly." She didn't want to explain, she just wanted to get out of his house.

"I need your help on something," he said conversationally. "It's just…I'm trying to understand what happened. You were there. Dad told me once when he first met Olivia it was love at first sight. Hers." He laughed harshly and looked at Madeline, "Those are his exact words."

"Well, that doesn't surprise me. She is a woman who knows what she wants."

"What happened when my father was shot?"

"I was there after your father was shot. I can tell you that Olivia tried to save him. I watched her try and save his life."

"The bullet nicked an artery, Dad bled out and had a heart attack. I talked to the coroner. There was no 'saving' possible. Just so I can understand since you and Olivia are friendly, what did the two of you talk about on the phone right before Dad was murdered?"

"Look Chase, I feel badly for you, but this conversation is—"

"The police told me the prosecutors would likely call you as a witness. I'm glad you'll be testifying at Olivia's trial."

"I can't really talk about that either." Madeline stood up again, "Sorry, but I do have to go, because—"

"I am looking forward to hearing about *everything* that went on between you and Olivia the day Dad was murdered."

"What do you mean?"

Chase said, his voice tight, "I think you know very well what I mean. Make no mistake, I intend to find out about you and Olivia and your little plan. The two of you had a secret, didn't you? I know you were hatching something together, weren't you? I'll find out, you know." He stood up and walked behind her chair.

Madeline half-turned and glanced at the door, only five feet away. She reached in her jacket pocket, palming her car keys.

"Tell me, why did Olivia believe she had to be so careful?" he abruptly demanded and slammed his water goblet down on the table so hard it broke, shards of glass skittering across the table. He brushed them to the floor.

She jarred her chair back and stood up, facing him, holding her computer bag. "Look, Chase, I don't know what you're talking about. I am very sorry about your father, but it's time I left. I'm expected back at the store in half an hour, so I'm in a bit of a rush. I'll be in touch with your appraisals."

Without another word, she walked to the door then down the hall and out the front door to her car. She looked back, Chase stood in the doorway, watching her with hooded eyes

Well, that was almost a disaster she thought as she slid into her car, the man was text book volatile. The good part was that she was now definitely and definitively done with checking into Harley's murder.

Let the cops figure out for themselves they'd made a big mistake.

Chapter Ten

A t home later that afternoon, Madeline called Olivia. This would be her last phone call. A goodbye call, more or less, although she wouldn't phrase it that way. The truth was there was nothing more she could do. At least Olivia had been released on bail.

"Hi, Olivia, I am so sorry to hear that you were arrested, but I'm glad to know that you're out now. The whole ordeal must be awful for you. What a terrible thing to happen, it just should not have happened. They've made a stupid mistake."

"Yes, I am living a nightmare. It is dreadful, really dreadful being booked and charged. But at least my lawyer was able to get me bailed out. All I had to do was come up with two million dollars!" she said ironically. "The only somewhat good news is that my lawyer continues to believe the state doesn't have a very strong case. He thinks the police were just anxious to make an arrest so the media would calm down. The police will probably use the time between now and the trial to, I don't know, try to dig up solid evidence because they don't have any now. You know Madeline there is no one I trust, except you."

Madeline sighed, "Well, since there isn't any evidence to find they'll come up empty. I thought I'd let you know I saw Chase this afternoon. I'm appraising Harley's watches for him."

"Harley had too many watches, and he really only ever wore one. I don't know why he wasted money on the others. You saw Chase? How is the 'dear' man?"

"He's convinced you are guilty. I tried talking to him about that, but he wouldn't listen."

"He hates me. A strong word, but he does."

"Anyway, I just wanted to let you know I heard that you had been arrested but I'm glad you've been released." She gave her only clue one last try. "This Wallace Wright who died in New Hampshire, you never heard Harley mention him?"

"Not that I remember. Why do you ask?"

"I had been thinking that maybe his death might be related to Harley's. But there doesn't seem to be any connection. I had a friend ask the New Hampshire cops about Wallace's death."

"Madeline, you are a dear friend to have done that for me. Thank you for that. What did the police say?"

And Madeline repeated word for word what Felix told her and their conclusion that Wallace had been shot by a person or persons unknown. She knew it was word-for-word because she'd pulled her notes out of her Harley file and read them out loud for Olivia.

"I guess the police really don't think they're related then," sighed Olivia. "You're sure?"

"Yes. Well, I should let you go. I am sorry that I wasn't able to be of much help. I am very, very sorry. If you think of anything I can do for you, just let me know."

"Goodbye, and Madeline, thank you for talking to your friend, and then to Chase, who can be a scary guy. I can't tell you how much I appreciate your concern and your friendship," and she disconnected.

* * *

Madeline stared at the phone, there was just one more call she had to make to wrap things up, this one to Felix. She felt like all she was doing lately was calling people on the phone.

"You may have heard that Olivia is now out on bail," she began.

"Of course," he said. "I work for a major newspaper, remember?"

"How could I have forgotten," she replied, stung. "It will be unlikely I can set up a time for you to talk to her. She won't want to talk to anyone about guns now."

"I wish you had set up a meeting before she was arrested."

Madeline wasn't about to apologize.

"You're still involved in this?" he asked.

"Well, no, not really. Not anymore."

"Fine then." He hung up without saying goodbye.

* * *

Madeline made herself a drink, a martini extra-dry with a twist, and went into her study. She pulled out her notes on Harley's watches, and referencing her chart, started to work on her appraisal of his collection. She leaned back when she got to the photos of Harley's Grand Complications Patek watch. Whatever Harley had done to have merited a $400,000 watch from his father must have been something pretty big. Madeline read the inscription on the back again and wrote down the date, February 8, 2002, and the words, *You Got Us Out, Son! Love, Dad*.

From the wording of the inscription, it did not seem to have been a sentimental present, so years ago Harley had done something very significant at Atherton Global. She stared at the date. Wallace would have been working at Atherton Global at the time, so he would have probably known. Penelope would have definitely known.

Madeline spent another hour preparing her appraisal for Chase, but she kept coming back to Harley's gold Patek with the inscription. She couldn't stop wondering what Harley had done that had so impressed his father. Penelope would probably know about the watch, and Madeline looked at the clock. It was only 8:00, not too late to call. This would definitely, absolutely be her last phone call about Olivia and Harley, so she pulled up Penelope's number and called her. But Penelope didn't answer, and Madeline didn't leave a message.

Madeline watched the news, national not local because she didn't want to listen anymore to news about Olivia's arrest, and then she went to bed.

She called Penelope's cell phone three times the next morning, but again no answer.

Madeline called her office in the afternoon, but Penelope didn't pick up the phone at her desk either and she left another message, asking her to call her back.

But Penelope never called Madeline back that afternoon. Or ever.

Chapter Eleven

Madeline's cell rang at 6: 05 am the next morning. She thought it was Abby with bad news. It wasn't Abby, it was Donia calling with bad news.

Donia began, "I thought you'd like to know, a woman who was Harley Atherton's assistant drowned yesterday. A Penelope Harwich."

Madeline gripped the phone. "What? Penelope? Drowned?"

"Yes. So you did know her. Penelope's body was just found off the beach near Cohasset. I just heard it on my police scanner. Once a cop always a cop I guess."

"You are sure Penelope Harwich is dead?"

"Police are usually quite exact about things like that, so yes, Penelope Harwich is dead."

"I've been trying to reach her by phone."

"Well, that would explain why she didn't pick up. I thought you were off the case."

"I am."

"Good."

"How? How did it happen?"

"I have no idea. It will be winter next month, so she wouldn't have been swimming."

"She was a kayaker. She must have been out in her kayak."

"Could be. Anyway, I thought I'd let you know before you heard about it on the news."

"Thank you for that, I appreciate it." Madeline disconnected.

Madeline made a pot of coffee and went online to *The Globe's* website. With a heavy heart, she read that Penelope's mother had reported her missing to the Coast Guard after sunset when she hadn't returned from kayaking off Hull. At 5:00 pm Penelope's car had been located, parked in Nantasket Beach's parking lot. When her body washed ashore ten hours later, she was wearing a life jacket, and authorities speculated she had been thrown out of her kayak in the choppy ocean and drowned.

The short article ended with the information that the Coast Guard was continuing their search for her kayak.

* * *

Madeline sent Olivia a text, saying she had just heard the sad news about Penelope, and Olivia called her immediately.

"My lawyer called me about Penelope ten minutes ago. I can't believe it, what a shock. Harley would have been devastated, absolutely devastated. They'd worked together for years, you know."

"Yes, she told me."

"That's right, you went to her condo in Cambridge, didn't you?"

"Yes." Madeline couldn't resist adding, "You asked me to find her, and I did. Although I don't think I mentioned she came in the store the same day you and Harley were in to look at the two necklaces. She bought a watch from me when she was there, a Patek. And I also spoke to her at Harley's wake."

"I always liked Penelope. She was so devoted to Harley, and it's all just so sad. Madeline, I could use a little company right now. Your place is at the Seaport, right? I was wondering, would it be alright if I dropped by? I've been staying at the InterContinental so I'm not that far away."

"Of course."

Fifteen minutes later, the concierge buzzed Madeline that Olivia was on her way up to her condo. When Olivia walked in the two women hugged, and Madeline led her to the living room.

Olivia sat in a brown wicker chair. "You have a nice place. I really like your table in the dining room."

"Thanks. My ex-husband picked it out. To be honest I should just give it to him. Tea?" she asked.

Olivia shook her head. "Just water would be good." She sighed. "What a tragedy about Penelope. I can hardly believe it. I know she loved kayaking. Harley gave her a new kayak last Christmas. It was pink, of course. She told him if she could she'd kayak around the world. What she loved the most was open-ocean kayaking. Harley told her a million times it was a crazy, dangerous sport, so I guess this tragedy is really not a surprise."

"Has someone from Atherton Global been in touch with her family?" asked Madeline.

"I called Edgar and asked him to get in touch with Human Resources and get her family's contact info," said Olivia. "I want to call them with my sympathies. I'll go to the service, too, where ever it's held, for Harley."

"You must be happy to be released."

There was a long silence, then Olivia said, "I thought it was interesting that as a condition of my bail the police took both of my passports, my French one, as well as my Tunisian one. I'm originally from Tunisia, you see. I have dual citizenship, which is convenient, sometimes. But since neither France nor Tunisia has an extradition treaty with the U.S. the police concluded I'm a flight risk. Anyway, ankle monitors are a thing of the past, but I do have to report, virtually which is great, to a probation officer every week on FaceTime since I am apparently a dangerous person. I can live with that, even though it is ridiculous."

Madeline took a bottle of Evian water out of the refrigerator, grabbed a glass, and set both in front of Olivia.

Madeline stood up and opened her front door to see if *The Boston Globe* had arrived. It had, and she flipped through it, and set it on the table. "There's nothing in the paper yet about Penelope. It's too soon I guess."

"My lawyer said the Coast Guard is searching for her kayak," said Olivia. "They may never find it, you know. I was told it could end up anywhere, possibly even in the Gulf Stream on its way to the UK. Or maybe it's sailing east to Portugal. The Coast Guard thinks though it probably got torn up by the rocks off Boston Harbor and sank to the bottom in the Atlantic." She ran her fingers through her hair and sighed. "You know my lawyer intended to call Penelope as a witness for the defense at my trial. He was going to have her testify to my undying love for Harley, or something to that effect. But now she can't."

There was a long silence, broken by Madeline. "How is the trial preparation coming?"

"My lawyer is trying to get the case thrown out before it gets to that, which would be a relief. He helped me arrange money for my bail with a line of credit on the house in Milton," said Olivia with a sad smile. "Harley left me well provided for, God bless him, and I can buy anything I want."

"A woman can't have too many emeralds." Madeline stopped and looked at her. "I'm sorry, Olivia, I didn't mean that you should buy more emeralds, I only meant—"

"I know what you meant. I miss Harley desperately, he always knew what to do. I can't believe he's gone forever, but there is nothing I can do about that." Olivia looked away and then looked back at Madeline, her eyes glistening with tears. "Edgar was supposed to be leaving for Paris on business, but I talked him into postponing his trip. I told him I needed him here."

"I'm glad that he's being helpful."

"Yes." Olivia leaned forward. "By the way, and I guess I'm not surprised, Chase will be testifying for the prosecution if there is a trial. Frankly, I'm worried that he and his buddies at Atherton Global will manufacturer some damning evidence and plant it somewhere. Or..." her voice trailed off.

"Or what?"

"Or, I don't know, they might..." Her voice trailed off again and she looked away and then back at Madeline. "I can hardly believe that dear Penelope is dead. Anyway, I need to get back to my hotel. I'll be moving to a new one tomorrow. These days, when I wake up in the morning it takes me a couple of seconds to remember which hotel I'm in."

"Why do you need to change hotels again?"

"Like I said, I'm careful. Don't listen to me, I'm just rambling. Well, I should be leaving."

Madeline walked Olivia down to the lobby and then down Channel Center

Street to her car.

They hugged, and Madeline stood on the sidewalk until Olivia was in her car and had turned onto rush-hour-busy A Street. Madeline waited until the taillights of her BMW disappeared in traffic.

Olivia had put on a brave front, but she had been more than just shocked by Penelope's death. Madeline had the sense that she was afraid.

* * *

Back inside her condo, Madeline walked up and down, she was nervous, edgy even, and with a cup of green tea, she went into the dining room. She was anxious about Olivia, even though she'd told herself she was done helping her. Madeline idly ran her fingers across the grain of the table. It was a nice table, and Felix had always loved it. Yes, she should definitely give it to him as a thank you for helping her. The gesture should make him happy since he'd pretty much hung up on her the last couple of times.

She thought again about Harley's murder, and Madeline could feel herself getting drawn back in, because Olivia was not safe, not at all. And Penelope's death had unnerved her. There was something 'off' about Harley's murder. The police had immediately jumped to the conclusion that Olivia killed Harley, influenced of course by Madeline's damning testimony, and they wouldn't let go of it.

As she sat there thinking about Harley's murder, the whole thing just didn't make sense. She had to admit that it did at first, and then, well, it didn't. What was she missing?

There was the mystery man, or possibly woman in brown that Olivia had spotted. That person, with an unknown motive, could have rowed up and shot Harley and then rowed away. So, who did Olivia see? It could have been anyone, even someone Madeline didn't know.

She knew it wasn't Penelope because she had been with Wallace's widow the afternoon Harley was shot. Edgar was there at the scene of the murder too, so it could have been him. Edgar was very friendly with Olivia, a little too friendly? He had been more or less at her beck and call. But more important, he was a former SEAL, trained within an inch of his life. It could definitely have been Edgar.

And then, of course, there was Chase.

At that moment an odd thought flashed into her brain, and all that was missing from the moment was a clap of thunder.

What if that horrible afternoon in Milton when Harley had been shot, it had been a mistake? An accident by the murderer? What if Harley had not been the intended victim? What if...what if Olivia, not Harley, had been the target? What if the murderer had intended to kill Olivia?

Who would want to kill Olivia? Chase of course. He hated her, but enough to kill her?

Madeline sat at the table, staring at her vintage London train station clock on the wall, her thoughts racing. Olivia said she and Harley had been talking, and then she remembered she had left something in the oven and had turned abruptly and went around the corner toward the house. What if Chase had been aiming at Olivia, but then she'd stepped away, in a hurry, and Harley had what...turned toward her as she was leaving...and he had been hit with the bullet meant for Olivia? While overhead, a plane flew low in its standard noisy landing pattern, heading to Logan Airport.

Yes, that could have definitely happened.

Should she go to the police even though all Madeline had were suspicions, and not a shred of proof? The good part, though, was that she didn't need to actually have proof, all she had to have was a strong possibility of someone else's guilt to get the police to focus on anyone else besides Olivia.

If Chase had aimed at Olivia, but she'd suddenly pivoted, the bullet would have hit Harley and killed him. And, if Chase accidentally killed his own father instead of Olivia, that hate would turn into rage at his own mistake. He would be beside himself with fury. What would a man like Chase do? For one thing, he'd want to make absolutely sure that Olivia was convicted on First Degree Murder and sentenced to life in prison without the possibility of parole, guaranteeing that his mistake would never be revealed.

And then too, Chase had told the police that Harley and Olivia had been in a big argument right before Harley was shot. Which according to Olivia was a bald-faced lie, but cleverly pointed the finger of guilt right at Olivia, and away from him. Yes, Chase was quite a slick, clever guy.

Madeline googled second-degree murder in Massachusetts, which carried a life sentence, with the possibility of parole after fifteen years. If Olivia was charged and convicted of second-degree murder, she'd be branded as a convicted felon for the rest of her life. And Chase would get away scot-free with accidentally shooting his father.

Although, what if Chase decided to hedge his bets in case Olivia wasn't convicted of anything—why wouldn't Chase just have Olivia killed in a flawlessly planned 'accident' right away? After all, he had an employee base of men who knew how to plan and execute 'accidents.' The investigation would probably come to an abrupt end with Olivia's death, and Chase in that case would also get away scot-free.

Under either scenario, a conviction or her 'accidental death,' Olivia was in serious jeopardy, and potentially in immediate danger. She wished now the police did actually have Olivia under surveillance. The problem was no one knew they should be concerned about something happening to Olivia. Except her.

Madeline sighed, her thoughts continuing to race. Felix had been right, the murderer was still out there, and she was sure it was Chase. She shivered, but not from the cold. She picked up her phone and called Donia, who used to track down murderers for a living. She would know what to do. But she only got Donia's recorded voice, saying that she was away and not reachable by cell phone, and would be back in a week.

In a week? There was a chance Olivia could be dead in a week.

Madeline wondered if she should call Olivia and let her know about her suspicions but decided against it. Suspicions are just flimsy suppositions. No, it wouldn't do any good, possibly even make things worse if she told Olivia that she was in danger. Besides, Olivia already sensed that.

She wished she could talk to Felix about this. Too bad she couldn't call him, although maybe...No, absolutely not, she couldn't call him, not in a million years. The last couple of times she'd spoken with him their conversations hadn't exactly ended well; he'd hung up on her. However, this was an emergency. She started to punch in his number to text him, then disconnected, thought about it, and started to text him again. Again, she accidentally hit disconnect.

She took a deep breath, and slowly put in his number one more time, and sent him a quick text. "Can I come and see you, please? I would like to talk, in person for just a couple of minutes."

Ten long minutes passed before he texted her back, "I'm at home, but come right over, I'll be here for another hour and then I leave for Holyoke," and he listed his address in Cambridge, on Bigelow Street, just a couple of houses down from where they'd lived when they were married.

* * *

Twenty minutes later Madeline parked her car in front of Felix's place, a narrow, two-story Victorian with any ornate molding stripped from the exterior years ago. Now it was just an ordinary old house. She was lucky to find a parking space on their old always-crammed-with-parked cars-street. She glanced over at her and Felix's old place five doors down. The converted carriage house was still lovely, and she felt a flash of regret. For the house.

She got out of the car and walked up the old, familiar sidewalk to Felix's new home. He opened the door before she could push the doorbell.

"Do come in. Welcome to my humble abode," he said.

She walked in, his house was newer than their old one, but inside his place had a standard boring layout, with not even a fireplace to add a flicker of interest. The living room did have gleaming cherry-wood floors, but the beige sofa and chairs were functional and unremarkable, and the small TV was likely never watched. There was nothing on the living room walls, they were completely bare. This place was perfect for Felix because he didn't really care where he lived, since he was rarely home. She looked around, so where was his elaborate Klipsch surround sound system? It must be in the bedroom. Where she would never set foot.

"I like your floors," she said.

He laughed. "Thanks, it's the only thing I've had done to the place. What would you like, a martini or coffee?"

She laughed. "At a quarter to nine in the morning? I'll go with, let me think for a minute...coffee, thank you."

He flicked on the light in the kitchen, and she heard him opening and closing cupboard doors. And then the whir of a coffee machine.

He walked back in with a cup of coffee on a tray and a container of cream and set it on the table beside her. "Sorry, no cappuccino today, or ever. It causes cancer, you know."

"I did not know that. And thanks, this is perfect."

Felix sat on a chair beside her. "And to what do I owe the pleasure of your visit?"

"Dead people. There are too many dead people in my life right now."

"Well, that's a conversation starter if there ever was one. How many do you have?"

"Three."

"Three. Let's see, there's the Wallace guy and then Harley. Who's the third? I know it's not your pal Olivia or I would have heard."

"Harley's assistant, Penelope, just died. She went out in a kayak on the Atlantic and drowned."

"Was it accidental?"

"Well, yes, I am assuming so."

"And you wanted to see me because..."

"Well, Harley's murderer is still out there, as you pointed out once, and I am afraid Olivia might be in danger, and there's nobody who's..."

Felix sighed, "So exactly what is it that you want me to do?"

"Could you, would you...I will owe you forever if you could just check..."

"No."

"No what?"

"I'm not going to check with my sources, or with any of my contacts. Besides none of them, to the best of my knowledge, are homicidal, or consort with people who have that tendency. At least lately."

"I think that Harley's murderer might have actually meant to..."

He interrupted brusquely, "Wait a minute, I thought you weren't involved in that anymore. At least that's what you told me."

Felix was being decidedly unhelpful.

"Well, it's just that I now think that there was a mistake, and…well, do you have a high-level contact in the Massachusetts state police?"

Felix thought for a minute. "No," he said, irritated.

Seconds ticked by, and then Madeline said, "I thought you were in love with me. Or something." A conversational gambit, since Felix liked to be surprised. This time he was, but not in a good way.

Felix laughed out loud. "You are a piece of work, aren't you?"

"Yes."

He laughed again, a hard laugh now. "I don't have time for this. I don't have time for any of this." He looked at her, his blue eyes cold, and flat.

Felix stood up and started to pace in his living room, his face rigid in anger. "You know, Madeline, for years you gave me a hard time about my work, and especially about the time I spent with my sources and my contacts in law enforcement and in government. You resented every second, every damn second I spent with them. But big surprise, after we're divorced and I've come back to Boston, you suddenly realize they might be useful to you. And so now you keep coming back to me for what you said you hated about my job, my sources, and my contacts. It seems you can't get enough of them, can you? So no, I won't help you. We really are, as you so eloquently put it, 'finito.'"

She'd definitely burned her bridges with Felix, although totally incinerated was more like it.

Madeline glanced at her watch, "Well, mercy me, just look at the time." She stood up, walked to the front door, and opened it.

"Sorry for the bother," she said over her shoulder and left.

She got in her car. She couldn't blame Felix. Well, she could a little, but the conversation had totally gone off the rails. She hadn't been able to get to the part where she thought Chase had intended to murder Olivia but had accidentally killed his own father. And Chase was likely now out to frame Olivia. Felix would have been interested in hearing all of that. She knew he would have.

She thought about walking back up the sidewalk ringing Felix's doorbell and explaining that to him. But she couldn't, his words had been too raw. She couldn't go back.

Madeline started her car and drove across Massachusetts Avenue into Boston. She was sad, but there were no tears. She had no tears when she divorced Felix, and she certainly wasn't about to sniffle now.

When she was driving down Boylston Street a tear did slowly fall down her cheek, but she brushed it away. Allergies she decided.

* * *

It was 9:15 by the time Madeline got to the store, and she had to rush setting up the jewelry displays. She didn't have time for even half a cup of coffee. She was almost done when Martin walked in.

"Can you take over?" she asked. "I have to send off a big appraisal, and I have to follow up on about thirty emails."

She didn't wait for him to reply but went to her desk in the back. She pulled up her Patek watch appraisals for Chase and spent several hours online checking recent sales of Patek's at auction and editing the document. She went over it three times and satisfied, she turned the fifteen-page appraisal into a PDF. There was no way she would hand-deliver it. Email would be better, so she drafted an email to Chase, friendly but not too friendly, attached the PDF, and hit send. She spent the next hour checking out upcoming jewelry auctions but found it hard to focus.

She stared at her computer. She needed to flesh out her 'Chase Killed His Own Father by Mistake' theory, and put it down on paper, and then take it to the police. The only person she hadn't talked to who'd been at the scene of the crime was Edgar, taciturn, steely-eyed, mono-syllabic Edgar. She should talk to him first to flesh out her theory since maybe he knew something that he didn't think was important about Chase? After all, the two men had been together at Harley's the day of his murder. So yes, she'd talk to Edgar. She needed a reason to talk to him though, a good one.

But what would make him want to talk to her in the first place? Maybe if he thought she had information about Harley's murder that the police didn't have? She didn't but, he would likely agree to meet with her if he was under the impression that she did.

Which was almost as good as actually having information.

Madeline called Atherton Global, but Edgar was out of the office for the next two days. Madeline did not leave a message because he might never call her back. She'd just have to wait until he returned and then get him on the phone.

* * *

The last thing Madeline wanted to do the next morning was fly to New York for the Art Deco jewelry auction. The problem was she'd already changed her mind three times, and if she changed it for a fourth Abby would be royally pissed. Madeline flew out at 8:00 am on the shuttle, anxious to get to the gem auction in Manhattan, and anxious to get back, and do more work on her big theory. And get ready to talk to Edgar.

She landed in New York only thirteen minutes late, and grabbed a cab to mid-town Manhattan, home of the Diamond District, one of the world's busiest gem and jewelry centers, squeezed between Fifth Avenue and the Avenue of the Americas.

The Diamond District was only a block from Rockefeller Center, but a world away in terms of its trade. Nearly 3,000 small businesses, a number of them tiny, were crammed into an area of less than fifteen square blocks that included gem dealers, wholesalers, retailers, stone cutters, fabricators and designers. The Diamond District was a thriving part of Manhattan, one that generated over four hundred million dollars in sales. Every single day.

The Diamond District looked, functioned, and sounded like an Old World bazaar, the streets literally thronged with sellers hawking their wares on sidewalks, and buyers crowding around displays or disappearing into narrow, dark storefronts. In the Diamond District, everyone seemed to be shouting and in a hurry.

For Madeline, it was like coming home, if home resembled a colorful 15th century medieval fair, minus midgets and draft horses.

She pushed her way down 47th Street, showed her badge to a security guard, passed through a metal detector, and was ushered into a small auditorium, with about fifty people, almost all of them gem dealers, the usual mix of Orthodox Jews, Iranians, South East Asians, and bored New Yorkers. She knew more than half by sight, and twenty by name, but she had no interest in talking to any of them.

Madeline bid aggressively and ended up with twenty superb Bakelite bracelets and necklaces, spending $20,000 for the whole lot. She was thrilled but tired and made it to La Guardia just in time for the 4:00 p.m. shuttle back to Boston. She called Martin to let him know she was on her way back to the store, but he didn't pick up. Which was good, it meant there were customers in the store.

The shuttle took off on time and Madeline tried to relax. At 25,000 feet she tried out a new tube of lipstick she'd just bought at the airport, a deep, vibrant red, and studied herself in her compact. Perfect.

Chapter Twelve

Madeline took an Uber from Boston's Logan Airport and replied to eight emails as she was driven to Coda Gems, hitting 'send' on the last one as the car pulled up in front of the store. When she opened the car door she saw two police cars pulled up in front of Coda Gems, their blue and red lights flashing. What was going on? She slammed the car door shut behind her and hurried inside, ignoring the hand-made Closed sign.

Two cops were standing by the front glass counter, talking to Martin, while a third was on his cell phone. Martin looked up when she came in and walked up to her.

"Don't worry," he said. "There was an attempted robbery this afternoon, but everything is fine. They didn't get anything." Martin turned to one of the cops and said, "This is Madeline Lane, one of the owners."

Only then did Madeline notice that Martin had a red, raw scrape on his jaw, and the beginning of a black eye. And then she saw a couple of bar stools along the side glass counter had been knocked over, and two chairs by the window were tipped over.

"Two guys came in about two hours ago," began Martin. "Fortunately three customers had just left." He lightly touching the scrape on his jaw and winced. "One of the robbers had a gun, but I was forty feet from the alarm. I knocked the gun out of his hand, and he hit me. Then, I grabbed this," Martin picked up what Madeline had always thought was his umbrella from the counter. It wasn't an umbrella.

He pulled off the blue nylon sheath, and Madeline stared at what was

134

basically a metal three-foot-long cudgel with metal rings at the top. He told her, "This is what is known in Buddhist circles as a 'khakkhara.' My father spent a lot of time in Thailand as a spice trader when I was young, and most of his friends were Shaolin Buddhist monks. Who all were, oddly enough, a bunch of really tough guys, who taught my father 'stick fighting', one of the oldest forms of martial arts. They gave him this stick when he got his Black Belt in Khakkhara, and he started giving me lessons when I was fourteen.

"It took me about five years before I was any good," said Martin as he charged across the store with tremendous speed, whipping the cudgel in front of him from left to right, each of his lightning strokes followed up with quick, powerful jabs. Martin's face was impassive, his feet in constant motion. He adjusted his balance with his left arm at every thrust, like a fencer. It was beautiful, and menacing at the same time.

"The key is to know exactly where to hit on the body for maximum effect. I practice khakkhara at least an hour every day to keep my form perfect. And it is. Anyway," Martin said, "two guys came to rob the store, but both of them are in the hospital now."

One of the policemen laughed. "I'm sure with multiple broken bones. They had to be carried out on stretchers. They're in Shattuck Hospital's Correctional Unit Wing, and I'm guessing in great pain."

Martin straightened his blue glasses, the cudgel in his right hand. "If you know what you're doing, you can incapacitate someone in about ten seconds with this. Or kill them."

Madeline, for one of the few times in her life, was speechless.

Martin pulled the nylon sheath back over his cudgel, carefully straightened the fabric, and his fighting stick became an umbrella again. The top was a bit thick and unwieldy now that she knew what it was, but it could pass for an umbrella.

"Good grief, Martin," said Madeline. She walked up to him and gave him a hug. "But you are fine?"

Martin laughed. "Better than fine. I enjoyed it, in a meditative, Buddhist way of course." He smiled.

"One of them pulled a gun on you?" said Madeline.

"Yes. But he didn't know how to handle a gun, I could tell by the way he held it, so it was easy to knock it out of his hand. I had him down on the floor in about a second with my stick. The other guy, well, he was going to run out the door so I took him down too. And then I locked the door so no customers would walk in on this, and I called 911. The police showed up, and then two ambulances took them away."

"Handcuffed, of course," said the other officer. "We have their gun in our cruiser."

The cops looked at Martin with respect, and one of them said to Madeline, "Martin is going to come down to the station and give us a demonstration of stick fighting next week. The guys will love it."

"You are a hero," she said to Martin.

"Yes, I am," said Martin simply. "You know, I've been carrying my stick around with me for years, but I've never had to use it before. It definitely came in handy today."

Madeline didn't know whether to laugh or hug him again, so she did both.

Martin agreed to come down to the police station later and give a statement, and the three policemen left after they had Madeline take a photo of them with Martin. Blue glasses and all. They wanted him to be holding his stick in the picture, but he said no.

"Martin, you surprise me," said Madeline after the door had closed, "Somehow, I thought of you as a ballroom dancer."

He shrugged, "Well I do know the rhumba, and the cha-cha-cha, and the foxtrot too of course. I am quite good."

"I am sure you are."

* * *

After they closed the store Madeline took Martin out for a drink at The Newbury Boston, across the street, and she had him tell her the whole story again from start to finish. At one point, he told her, his blue glasses had gotten knocked off, which had infuriated him. "They are Alexander McQueen, you know," which apparently explained his anger.

136

She told Martin he didn't need to come in the next day, but he insisted he was alright, and he wanted to come to work, so she said that would be fine. For the first time, Madeline would be glad to see him.

* * *

Madeline called Abby when she finally got home that night.

She started out, "Martin is fine, the store is fine, nothing was stolen while I was in Manhattan," and told her about the attempted robbery. As expected, Abby was shocked, and Madeline reassured her Martin was alright. "He has a scrape on his jaw, a black eye, and there were a couple of stools and chairs knocked over and that was it."

Abby said, "You're telling me that two men walked in with a gun, and Martin sent both of them to the hospital, with just a stick?"

"It's called a stick, but it's metal, and quite deadly."

"Good grief, this is unbelievable. Incredible. I'm glad you weren't in the store."

"Actually, I'm not, I'm sorry I missed it. Martin was apparently magnificent. I would have liked to see him in action."

"Madeline, this isn't funny," said Abby. "Someone could have been seriously hurt, or even killed. I still can hardly believe it. I was concerned that it might happen, and now it has."

A pause, then Abby said, "You know, I think it's time I came back to Boston. Mom doesn't really need me, since Dad has a nurse coming in again, so I'll talk to him and find out what is a good day for me to come back. Can you give me Martin's phone number? I want to call him."

Madeline gave her the number, saying, "Abby, you don't need to come back to Boston early, but it sounds like you want to. When you do, I will be so very glad to see you. Very glad."

"You're absolutely sure Martin is fine?"

"He said he was, and he looked alright to me, except for being banged up a little bit. I'll check with him again tomorrow morning. Did you know he is a ballroom dancer? That's what he said anyway. I'll ask him to show me the foxtrot and that way I'll know for sure."

"I'll let you know what day I'll be coming back," said Abby. "And I am glad that Martin is fine, Coda is fine, and you're fine."

Madeline wasn't so sure about her being 'fine'. At least she hadn't worried about Olivia or Chase for the last six hours.

The two partners said goodnight and they hung up.

* * *

Even though it was late she sent a 'checking in' text to Olivia, who shot back an immediate reply, "I am as well as I can be, given the situation. I was followed home again tonight."

Which was both bad and good. At least she knew Olivia was alive.

Madeline replied to her text, "If you want company, I can come over."

Olivia's reply was short and definite. "Thanks, I am fine. You are kind to be thinking of me."

* * *

The next morning Martin walked into the store just as Madeline finished setting up the displays, as usual carrying his "'umbrella'," tucked under his arm. She was surprised she'd ever thought it was an average umbrella because if one looked at it closely, even covered again in a blue nylon sheath, it was just a bit too wide at the top because of the metal rings.

Martin did seem alright, except his black eye was bigger, and blacker.

"I talked to Abby last night," she told him as he put his coat, boots, and 'umbrella' in the closet. "She's coming back tomorrow, but we still want you to come in for the rest of this week."

Martin smiled. "Yes, I'll be happy to come in, and it will be good to see her. She called me last night, and we talked for an hour. She was very concerned."

Madeline handed him the heavy leather bag of Art Deco jewelry she'd bought in the Diamond District the day before. "I've already inventoried these, but you can set up the display if you like, but they should be in the front case since our customers have never seen them before."

Martin nodded, accepting her suggestion for what it was; a thank you and a peace offering. He still drove her crazy, but she'd just have to get used to it. She supposed she could do that.

She looked at him, and Martin's big blue glasses made his black eye even more noticeable. She took him into the alcove that served as their kitchen, had him take off his glasses, and pulled out a tube of matte makeup. She applied the makeup to the area around his right eye, blending it with her fingers, showing him how it was done and had him put on his glasses. His black eye was all but unnoticeable unless you were standing right in front of him. She dabbed some makeup on the scrape on his jaw and stood back.

"It's better," she said. "Look in the mirror. What do you think?"

He looked intently in the mirror above the sink. "I think I see a handsome roust-about staring back at me."

"I agree," and she handed him the tube of makeup. "Compliments of the house," she said, and he laughed.

* * *

After lunch, Madeline went over her notes on Harley's murder and started to set up a quick chart of the timeline of her 'Chase Killed His Own Father by Mistake' theory. Once she talked to Edgar she could plug in any new information. The police would have to be impressed.

When she finished, she sat back and carefully went over her chart.

After five minutes she knew her chart and her theory were both worthless. The whole thing had been a complete waste of time. If Chase had been successful and shot Olivia dead, with Harley still very much alive, he would have come at Chase like a charging bull and probably would have killed him. Plus, there were too many flukes in her brilliant hypotheses, which under scrutiny was based on a series of coincidences, and had a stitched-together feel. Yes, Olivia did leave something in the oven, and Chase not only hated his stepmother, he was also a bad shot, and then at just the right moment with no one else around, Chase just happened to find Harley and Olivia together on the patio. And then Chase took aim at Olivia and fired just as she happened to turn away. And what about the convenient low-flying plane in a usual loud and annoying landing pattern, which muted the sound of the gunshot and of Harley dropping to the ground?

Her theory was useless, she was grasping at straws to prove Chase's guilt. She was glad she hadn't told Felix because he would have dismissed her reconstruction as flimsy in two seconds.

Regardless, Madeline did hit 'Save' on her desktop and shoved the file into her now 'Harley Atherton' folder, filled with PDFs of news articles on his murder, Olivia's arrest, and the reports of Penelope's drowning in Hull. She turned off her computer and stared at the wall. She was still convinced Chase had murdered Harley, she just didn't have any proof or motive.

She finally shook her head, straightened her shoulders, and went out to wait on customers.

After the lunch hour rush, Madeline glanced at her calendar; Edgar was due back at Atherton Global today. But she had nothing to talk to him about now, not since her big, brilliant theory had gone up in smoke. Too bad, because she had been interested in talking to him. Edgar was there at the scene of the crime after all and certainly would have opinions about it. The man definitely had opinions about Wallace's old files, since he had told Chase quite clearly not to turn them over to the police. Why? Something had happened back then, but what? She knew then that she still needed to talk to Edgar. Those files of Wallace's were the only real lead she ever had. But why would Harley or anyone at Atherton Global have held onto actual paper files for so many years if they contained damaging information? Unless the person who'd kept them didn't understand the importance of the information. Then too, maybe the box of files had simply been forgotten as the company had grown year after year.

Madeline sat up with a start when she remembered a week and a half ago Penelope had said she and Wallace were supposed to have drinks together. Did Edgar know that? She bet he didn't.

She couldn't let go of Harley's murder, or rather she couldn't let go of trying to keep Olivia safe. It was like holding a tiger by the tail. If you let go of it you were dead. Madeline conveniently glossed over the alternative; if you held onto the tiger's tail you were also dead.

At the very least she should definitely have a quick chat with Edgar. Maybe he knew something about Chase and she might get a new perspective. Madeline decided a restaurant would be a good place to meet Edgar as she doodled on a pad of paper. How could she get him to agree to meet her with just a phone call? She would have to get his attention right away, and then keep it. Her original plan to hint to Edgar that she had information about Harley's murder would probably still work.

She had to be careful though, she didn't want it to sound like she was fishing for information. That would make him cagey. A good way to lead up to that would be by talking about Penelope. Yes, that would be perfect, that should throw him off balance.

Madeline couldn't pass up a chance to find out what Edgar knew. But first, she had to get him to agree to even meet with her.

Chapter Thirteen

Madeline went out front and told Martin she was about to get on an important call and couldn't be interrupted, then she shut the door to the office and picked up the phone. She told the receptionist at Atherton Global she needed to talk to Edgar about 'an important matter' and she was connected to him immediately.

Edgar came on the line immediately, "How can I help you, Madeline?"

"Do you have a minute? There's something I'd like to talk to you about. It's complicated."

"Yes, I have a minute."

"Well, I've been thinking about Harley's murder, and I was wondering if we could get together for just a half an hour this afternoon? I know it's short notice and I apologize, but I'd like to meet with you, sooner rather than later. Not at Atherton Global, but at a restaurant or someplace nearby. Just to talk."

"About what? "

"Like I said, it's complicated. I'd like to talk about information the police might not be aware of."

"Shouldn't you be talking to the state police about this?"

Madeline guessed that would be the first thing Edgar would say since he was a law-and-order type. "I thought about that, but no, not yet. I wanted to talk to you first. Alone." That last word was important. Madeline didn't want him to bring Chase.

"I see." She could hear Edgar shuffling some papers on his desk, then he said, "How about 3:00? Where do you want to meet?"

Good, she had definitely gotten his attention. "I was thinking Slap Jacks because it's close to your office."

There was a long silence. Finally, Edgar said, "Fine, I'll be there at three."

"Thank you, I appreciate it," she said, and they both disconnected.

Madeline told Martin that she had to leave at 2:30 for an important meeting, and a rush of customers came in then, and she sold two Tiffany necklaces and Martin sold a heavy Cartier estate diamond brooch, but she kept her eye on the clock the entire time.

Finally, it was 2:30 and as she left, Martin said, "Good luck."

"Thanks, I'll need it."

As she walked out the door she thought about Martin. He would be gone in a few days and she would miss him, her Ballroom-Dancing-Buddhist-Warrior. Which made her smile for the first time in a long time.

* * *

Edgar was waiting for her at Slap Jack's, sitting at a table by a window, with a view of a shimmering glass office building across the street, and a postage-stamp-sized parking lot beside it. He was dressed in camouflage and looked like a man about to set off on a covert mission any minute. She knew that was unlikely, he was probably just dressed for a training session.

A glass of seltzer water stood in front of him, a thin lemon slice abandoned on a napkin. He watched her cross the restaurant floor to his table, and he stood when she walked up.

"Thank you for coming," she said.

He nodded, and they sat down.

The place was almost empty, just a couple of men in suits in the back, drinking. Their waiter picked up empty glasses in front of them and set down fresh drinks. The men looked slightly drunk.

She sat down and beckoned the waiter over. "Coffee," she said, "black, please." She ordered that since serious people, like Felix, drank only black coffee.

The waiter came back immediately with her coffee and Madeline took one sip and set it back down. It tasted like tree bark. She stopped the waiter

143

and said, "I've changed my mind. Please bring me a cup of regular American coffee. With cream and sugar."

Edgar looked at her, waiting for her to begin.

She said, "It is a tragedy about Penelope."

"Yes, it is."

"I've been thinking a lot about her. About her relationship with Wallace Wright, the guy from Raytheon who used to work at…"

That got Edgar's attention, and his eyes flashed for a second and then went back to their usual impenetrable black. "I know who he is. What do you mean, 'her relationship'?"

"I stopped by Penelope's place in Cambridge a couple of days after Harley was killed. She talked about him, and Wallace too."

That surprised Edgar. "She did? Penelope talked about Wallace? What exactly did she say?"

"That he had called her and wanted to get together, so they set up a day and time to meet."

"And this was Wallace's idea, not hers?"

"Yes. Penelope said he wanted to talk, but he didn't say about what. So, they set up a time to meet for drinks, and two days later he's shot dead."

Edgar pushed away his glass of seltzer. "That's it? That's the information you said the police might not be aware of?"

"I believe it could be relevant."

He said dismissively, "Tell me why you are involved in this?"

"Me? I'm just very concerned that Olivia has been charged with Harley's murder, and I know she didn't kill him. I want the police to get their focus off Olivia and onto someone else. They should be concentrating on a real suspect who I think had a connection to Wallace." She didn't want to mention Chase, yet.

"And who might this person be?" Edgar hadn't moved a muscle since she'd sat down, he just watched her. She noticed he rarely blinked.

"I don't know, but it wasn't Olivia. Who do you think shot Harley?"

"What does it matter what I think? Back to Penelope, she didn't say what Wallace wanted to talk about?"

"Well no, not really."

Edgar said, an edge in his voice now, "What do you mean 'not really'?"

He looked at her, waiting for her to continue. That morning Madeline had gone over what she'd say to Edgar about ten times before she left to meet him. A meeting that had gone fairly well, so far. But now she was just winging it. Not a wise thing to do around Edgar.

Still, Madeline had to at least answer Edgar's question, so she said the first vague thing she could think of, "I had the sense it had to do with Harley. Something that happened a long time ago."

"Why? What gave you that sense?" Edgar leaned forward across the table, so close she could almost feel his breath. "What do you know?"

"Well, Penelope told me that Harley had made one or two mistakes in his life." She added, "Quite big ones."

Penelope didn't exactly say that, but that's what she must have meant. That should satisfy Edgar.

He looked at her, his dark eyes became even darker. He didn't say anything for several long seconds, then finally, "Madeline, what *exactly* do you know?"

She shrugged, "About what?"

"What Harley and Wallace were up to twenty years ago. It's political dynamite, even now. Maybe even more so. What else did Penelope say?"

"Look, Edgar, I've told you everything I can remember that Penelope said. I didn't want to press her, she was crying when she talked about Wallace." That wasn't true, but it should keep Edgar quiet for at least a minute until she figured out a good way to get out of the restaurant and away from his questions. Edgar hadn't taken his steely eyes off her since she walked in the door. It was time for her to leave since she wouldn't get any concrete information out of Edgar. Edgar was the type to take in information, not give it.

A brilliant thought struck her and she suddenly grabbed her cell phone out of her purse, looked at it, then at Edgar. "I'm sorry but I have to go back to the store. I just got a text, telling me to come back to the store *immediately*." Madeline stood up. "Thank you for meeting me. If you don't mind, I'll call you later and we can talk some more."

145

She had no intention of ever calling him. Something had happened a long time ago, but whatever it was she had no way of getting it out of Edgar in a restaurant.

He picked up his drink, swirled the ice around in the full glass, and set it back down, "Take my advice and stay out of this," he said, without inflection.

She took out her wallet, but Edgar held up his hand, so she walked out the door. She got in her car, and since he was probably watching her now from the window by their table, she drove out of her parking spot and screeched her way down State Street. She had added the screeching part for Edgar's benefit. Nothing says 'immediate' like screeching tires.

* * *

Back at the store, Madeline thought about her meeting with Edgar for the rest of the afternoon. She hadn't learned anything, except that he was very concerned about something that Wallace and Harley had done a long time ago. 'Political dynamite' he'd said. It was too bad Penelope had been above gossip, which was almost funny because she hadn't been above sleeping with the boss.

The rest of the day dragged until it was time for her and Martin to close up. She drove home and parked her car in the underground garage at her building in her spot way in the back. Then, as she was walking to the elevator, she thought she heard footsteps behind her. She turned quickly but didn't see anyone. Maybe she was mistaken? She stopped and peered into the dark garage but didn't see or hear anything. Then, the elevator chimed as the door jarred open and four residents walked out to their cars, talking and laughing loudly. She was relieved and ran up to the door, making it inside the elevator just as the door was closing.

Back now in her unit on the eleventh floor, she ordered a pizza and went to her desk in her study. Her meeting with Edgar hadn't been of any real help, there were too many things she just didn't know. She opened her Harley folder. She wrote up a memo of her meeting with Edgar, and dropped it in the folder.

Unfortunately, she had no idea what to do next. Then Donia called her.

* * *

"Maybe I shouldn't be telling you this," began Donia, but I heard it from an old friend in the Coast Guard, and it will be on the internet and TV shortly, so I can give you an update, in good conscience."

"So, tell me."

"Well, the Coast Guard did find that woman's kayak, the one you knew who worked for your dead guy? They found it stuck in a rocky cove, off Cohasset. And it was in pretty good shape, except for a big hole just under the seat."

"What? Well, that's good news I guess that they found it. But a hole?"

"Well, I'm not sure if it is good news. The big hole was not the usual kind of hole you'd find in a kayak. They're made out of a composite these days, which includes resin, so it's very tough stuff, and they're manufactured to take a lot of wear and tear. They can get banged around and torn up by rocks, and I was told the big hole was a bit jagged, but only in spots. Basically, it looked like the hole had been man-made. And then, as near as they can figure, the hole had been badly patched over with composite. The patched hole was under the seat, so it would have been hard to see unless you were looking for it."

"Man-made? Why would there be a man-made hole in a kayak?"

"You have one guess," said Donia. "Remember, I was a homicide investigator for years.

"Someone wanted Penelope dead?"

"Bingo, you win The Murder Business prize of the week. Like I said, it was patched over, but it was a bad job, superficial only, not good enough to hold in rough, bad weather, and maybe that was on purpose. The woman goes out on a relatively calm day it's fine, but in very rough seas, the patch doesn't hold, the kayak sinks and she drowns."

"But why? Why would anyone do that? Is there any proof?"

"No, there is no proof, but it's unlikely the woman made a hole in her kayak herself. So maybe somebody put a hole in Penelope's kayak on purpose, and then that same somebody did a very bad job of patching it. It's true Penelope could have patched it up herself, but if she did, she did a terrible job. That kayak should never, ever have been taken out in open ocean in bad weather. It would have been stupid, and dangerous. Anyway, Penelope did go out in bad weather, and the force of the winds and the tide ripped the patch off. The kayak took on water, sank, and she drowned."

"Even with a life jacket?"

"Yes. Life jackets can keep your body on top of the water, but they won't necessarily keep your head above water, especially in rough swells."

"What will happen next?"

"The Coast Guard is launching an investigation now, with the state police. Where did Penelope keep her kayak?"

"I have no idea."

"Well, the police will find out and talk to people and get whatever information they can. The whole thing is suspicious and doesn't seem accidental to me, but it will be almost impossible to prove otherwise. Unless, of course, a witness comes forward who saw someone drilling a hole in her kayak. Don't get your hopes up though that that will happen."

Madeline sighed. "This is sad as well as frightening news."

"I'm glad for your sake that you're well out of this. Anyway, I thought you'd want to know."

"Thank you for telling me, I appreciate it." Madeline hung up.

For a moment Madeline did wonder if Penelope's death was connected to Harley's murder. And Wallace's too. But only for a second.

Of course, they were connected.

It was time she stopped whirling around, talking to people, stirring things up, and being of no help to Olivia. Besides, there wasn't anyone left she could talk to anymore. She could talk to Olivia again, but that would only frighten her.

What about that person that was walking up behind her in the garage? That had been really spooky if there actually had been someone walking behind her. She wasn't sure now. There was a part of Madeline that wanted to go back down to the garage and just have a look around. The stupid part. She didn't go down to the garage.

Still, if someone had been waiting for her in her garage, that meant someone had known her movements, knew approximately when she came and went. Could this be related to her meeting with Edgar?

Just to be on the safe side she would take an Uber to the store the next morning. And even though Abby was coming back, she'd tell her she definitely wanted to keep Martin on for more than just a week.

Madeline turned on the TV and watched a rerun of *Law & Order*. The episode held her interest for all of five minutes. Her own life had too much crime drama already, and she couldn't relate to the made-up kind.

Chapter Fourteen

Madeline was up early the next morning and was at the store by 7:30, because the big day had finally arrived, Abby was coming home. She was landing in Boston at 8:45 am. At least for now Madeline had to forget about old plots and recent murders. She had a business to run. Edgar had been right, she needed to stay out of Atherton Global's business.

By 8:25 the dozen long-stem yellow roses Madeline had ordered the day before had been delivered and were in a crystal vase on Abby's desk. And she'd already taken their jewelry out of the safe and had all the displays set up in their glass cases.

Martin walked in at 9:00, and Madeline was still going up and down along their counters, making little adjustments to the displays. At 9:55 Martin said to her, "I need to point out that is the third time you've changed the ruby and the diamond layout since I've been here this morning."

"Is it? I guess you're right. Abby should have been here by now. Where is she?"

"Her plane might have been delayed, or she's still at the luggage carousel, or she's stuck in traffic in the Ted Williams Tunnel. Why don't you have another cup of coffee? If you want my opinion, I think you need to be just a bit more wired."

Madeline ignored Martin and set to work, this time on the emerald display again, moving a chunky emerald bracelet to the center of the glass case, her head bent over the counter in concentration. She didn't hear the bells chime on their door when it opened, and she didn't hear Abby walk up beside her.

Abby said, "It looks perfect to me."

Madeline looked up, laughed, and gave her a big hug. "Thank God you're here, you're finally here. Welcome back. I missed you."

Abby kissed her on the cheek, "I missed you too, and I am so very, very glad to be back."

Martin walked over and Abby gave him a big kiss too and laughing, she said, "Alright, that's enough kissing for one day." She reached for his chin, and examined the scrape on his jaw, and then inspected his black eye. "Your make-up looks pretty good."

"It's Madeline's. She showed me how to apply it yesterday and she gave me a tube."

"Thank you again for what you did Martin," she said.

"My pleasure, sort of. I've never actually broken anyone's bones before."

"What did it feel like?" asked Madeline, and Abby grimaced.

"It was sort of like snapping a pencil," he said, "Actually, it wasn't, it wasn't loud at all. More of a 'thunk' and that was it. I thought it would be louder. I didn't know I'd broken their legs until I saw they couldn't walk."

"Let's talk about something else," said Abby. "It's over, and we are very lucky that Martin was here. I've already talked to Wentworth," and she turned to him, "they're our security company, and I'm having a new alarm system with five emergency call buttons installed throughout the store."

"Good," said Madeline. "The sooner the better. We could do with an extra layer of protection, because, well, you just never know."

Abby glanced at her but didn't say anything.

* * *

An older woman with silver hair and a silver leather jacket walked in the store, and Martin whispered, "I'll handle this," and the two partners went into the office and talked about launching a promotion for their new ruby collection.

"Abby, let's have Martin come in for another couple of months. We could use him since the Holidays are coming up and for our big promotion for Liz

Schuvart's rubies could start the beginning of December, and we'll run it through January and into Valentine's Day."

"Well, I suppose that is a good idea. I'll talk to him and see if he could come in three or four days a week for a couple of months."

Abby went to her desk and set up her laptop, and Madeline went out front to check on the jewelry displays for one last time. Martin was at the cash register ringing up the sale of a sterling silver necklace for the woman with silver hair.

Madeline was glad that life was returning to normal, even if she did know it was normal with a thin veneer.

There was a murderer, maybe even more than one, still out there.

* * *

A card from Chase came to the store for Madeline in the afternoon, thanking her for Harley's watch appraisals. On the inside Chase had written, "It was good of you to come to the house to appraise Dad's watches. It is much appreciated and was very helpful." He signed it, "With Kind Regards."

Chase wouldn't have ended his message with regards, much less, kind ones if he knew what she was really thinking.

Madeline showed the card to Abby. On the front and inside were watercolors of wildflowers, and Abby said, "That was a nice, courteous note. Why were you appraising Harley's watches?"

"I thought it would be helpful since his father had just died. I didn't charge him of course, and he appreciated the offer."

Abby raised her eyebrows, "Really? I'm glad. See, rich people aren't so horrible after all, are they?"

"Maybe," she said as she turned away. "I need to check the emerald display again," and she went out to the front of the store. Telling Abby that she really believed Chase, while he was indeed courteous, had just murdered his own father would not have been a good idea.

* * *

152

After they'd closed the store Abby and Madeline went across the street to the old Ritz Carlton for drinks. Abby as usual ordered a glass of chardonnay and Madeline ordered her standard gin martini, straight up, extra dry, and with a twist.

"Mom gets better every day," said Abby after the waiter walked away. "Although now that she has a history of heart problems it's still a worry. But the doctors are encouraged at how quickly she's recovering. Dad, well he pretends there's nothing terribly wrong with her, but he watches her like a hawk, which is good, I suppose. I just wish I lived closer, but Chicago is only a two-hour plane ride away, and I'll go back again over Christmas. Still, I am thinking of..." and Abby's voice trailed off.

Madeline froze. It had occurred to her that Abby might want to move back to Chicago to be closer to her mother, and her father too of course. Which from Madeline's standpoint would be a disaster, the total kind.

Madeline interjected, "That's good news that she is doing well, and I'm glad for them, and for you. Going back over Christmas is a good idea since a two-hour plane ride is nothing these days."

"I suppose you're right, Mom is already looking forward to my return. So how has everything been going? By the way, I was pretty shocked that Olivia Atherton has been charged with second-degree murder and is out on bail. That whole story is so sad. I hope you're not getting involved in—"

"Olivia's not guilty, you know, and she shouldn't have been arrested. I feel responsible and depressed. Take your pick. Oh, I forgot, helpless too."

"I am sorry about it, Madeline, but it's not your fault."

"Well, it sort of is, and if it weren't for me it might not have turned out this way."

"To be honest, I'm a bit worried that you might do something..."

"Stupid?" said Madeline.

"No, I was thinking more along the lines of 'ridiculously risky.'"

That made Madeline laugh out loud, "No worries. I've already done that."

Abby looked at Madeline, "What do you mean?"

"Nothing. Never mind. Life can get back to normal now that you're back. I hope."

* * *

That night, in her study, Madeline opened the Harley folder and started to go through it. She had the feeling that the answer was right in front of her, but she just couldn't see it.

She was relieved that Abby was back, although she would have to say something to her about Penelope in the next day or so. Abby only read *The Wall Street Journal* but it seemed likely that if Penelope's death would turn into a criminal investigation it certainly would be covered by Boston's local TV stations. She'd have to tell Abby before she heard it on the news.

Madeline sat scrolling through the files, and she printed color copies of the photos of Harley's 'Grand Complications' Patek, the one his father had given him in 2002. The watch that was appraised at $400,000. Why would a father give a son a watch that was worth as much as a house in a Boston suburb? Wallace had still been a financial officer at Atherton Global, so he would have likely known about the very expensive watch, and Penelope most certainly would have known. On the other hand, Edgar hadn't been there, he wouldn't have even been in college at the time. Did he know about it? Too bad she couldn't just call him up and ask him.

Madeline went on Google and plugged in Feb. 8, 2002, the date and year on the watch. She wasted twenty minutes scrolling through pages of worthless information like birthdays of celebrities.

She even tried Wikipedia but didn't find anything of possible significance that had happened on that date there either. Of course, the date was related to Atherton Global. Somehow.

* * *

Just after 2:00 there was a knock on Chase's office door.

"Come in," Chase said, and Edgar walked in.

Chase said, "I saw your email that you're not going to Paris, but that you'd sent Harold the new Operations guy instead?" Chase didn't bring it up, but Edgar should have cleared that with him first.

"Turns out it wasn't a good time to leave."

Chase nodded to the chair across from him, but Edgar said, "Let's go outside."

Chase stood up, so Edgar must not like being recorded, but why was he concerned about that now? He had to know Harley had recorded every conversation in his office for years. Except, unfortunately, not any phone calls about his mysterious trip to Paris, because he hadn't made any from his office. Chase followed Edgar to the elevator and down to the street.

Once on the sidewalk, Edgar led him to the restaurant Slap Jacks, and to a table in the back. The two men sat, and Chase looked around. "At least it's quiet here." They both ordered draft Heineken, and since they were the only customers, the waiter came back immediately with their order.

Edgar said, "Harold went to Harley's hotel yesterday in Paris. He talked to a couple of staff members, but none of them had any idea what Harley did the day he was there. All I know is that he went there to see someone who had something to show him, and that's it. I got a copy of Harley's car rental record, and he drove a total of twenty-seven miles, which tells me nothing. Harley might have left Paris, or he might not have.

"There is a chance Harley got a call from this mystery man right before he was killed since he was expecting a 'very important' call that day. Like I told you, I'm positive he had his cell phone in his hand when he was shot. A team of our engineers is still working on that phone, so there's a slight chance they can reconstruct where his calls came from that day. I'll let you know if they find anything."

"Good," said Chase.

"Do you still have a tap on Olivia's phone?"

"Of course. Believe it or not, that Madeline woman calls her regularly."

"What do they talk about?" asked Edgar, leaning forward.

"Just bullshit stuff. By the way, you've seen the reports on the tails on Olivia? She doesn't go anywhere, except to move to a different hotel almost every night."

"I asked her about why she was moving to different hotels all the time," said Edgar. "She said she likes the change."

155

"I noticed she calls you quite a bit."

Edgar shrugged. "She does."

"You've heard that the investigation into Penelope's drowning might become a criminal one?"

"Yes."

Chase said, annoyed by Edgar's abrupt answers, "So what do you think?"

"Me? I think somebody wanted her dead."

Chase said, "And exactly who do you think that somebody might be?" loud enough that their waiter by the cash register jerked up his head.

"Could be anybody. We need to do something about Madeline though," said Edgar. "I don't like her poking her nose in our business. I've had her under surveillance since yesterday afternoon."

"Get that stopped," said Chase. "Call that off immediately, it's just a waste of time and manpower. Have them concentrate on Olivia. I want all exits covered at whatever hotel she's staying at. I don't want her slipping out a side door somewhere and I don't know about it."

Edgar didn't say anything.

Chase checked Harley's gold watch on his wrist. "About Penelope, you have no idea who might have drilled a hole in her kayak?"

"Why are you asking me?" snapped Edgar. "Well, it was nice talking to you," and he stood up and walked out.

Chase stared after Edgar. He picked up the phone and told the leader of the team following Olivia that the surveillance on her needed to be 24/7. Olivia was bound to make a mistake sooner or later.

* * *

At home, Madeline went on three more search engines looking for information about the date on Harley's watch but didn't find anything that had a link to Harley or Atherton Global. She remembered Felix had said something about Harley and his father being involved in civil wars in the early 2000s in North Africa, and she tried to remember which countries. She remembered Algeria and Libya, but she couldn't remember the others. She could do a bit of reading on revolts and wars in those countries and with any luck find out if Atherton Global had been involved. She had to at least try. She took out the photos of Harley's gold watch, and re-read the inscription, written by Harley's proud father, who'd also been a bloody SOB, according to Felix.

Madeline went on Amazon and ordered two 20th century military histories, one on Algeria and the other on Libya, both out of print but still available as eBooks. Both of them showed up on her computer minutes later. She started with the Libya one, and for an hour scrolled through page after page of bombed-out buildings and sad-eyed men, but nothing fit. She looked at the clock, this was dreary and sad.

She clicked open the military history eBook on Algeria, a country rocked by conflict and bloodshed as well. Algeria had a couple of big wars, not only the big one of independence from France but a particularly violent and brutal one, the Algerian Civil War, of 1988 – 2002. Which was also known as the "Dirty War" because of its extreme violence and brutality towards the civilian population. So that could have been one of the civil wars that Harley and his father had been involved in. Hadn't Felix said that Atherton Global played a dangerous game back then, arming and training both sides in a conflict? Yes, even though they'd done that at different times that would still be dangerous. The first thing Madeline did was check the index, but Atherton Global wasn't listed, which actually wasn't a surprise. She'd read that private military contractors liked to keep a low profile; most of their business came from word of mouth.

Ten minutes later she read that foreign military contractors had been brought in by both the rebels and the government in the Algerian Civil War, and she sat up straight. Unfortunately, no company names were listed.

The eBook had a section in the back of Algerian Civil War photos, which were gruesome even in black and white. There was a second section of color photos at the end but she skipped those. She wasn't in the mood to look at more photos of pooling bright red blood from wounded or dead soldiers.

She went back to the front section of the book and read about their civil war, which ended on February 8, 2002. She had to read the date three times.

Bingo! That was the date of the inscription on Harley's watch.

Chapter Fifteen

Madeline leaned back in her chair, pleased that she'd solved the mystery of Harley's watch. Atherton Global had been involved in the Algerian Civil War. She read on about the conflict, a vicious and bloody one, with estimates of up to 200,000 civilian deaths. She was glad she hadn't paged to the color photos at the end.

* * *

Madeline did not take an Uber to the store the next morning because it was a waste of time. If she was being followed, whoever was behind it, and she suspected Edgar, that person knew what time she left and where she was going. Which meant a subterfuge would be unnecessary, so she boldly drove her reliable Audi to Coda Gems, keeping her eyes on her rearview mirror, but didn't notice anything unusual. She would be extra careful when she'd go to pick up her car that night and keep her cell phone in her hand when she left her car in her building's garage, and she'd be just fine.

She was in the store that morning at her usual 8:00 am, and an hour later Martin and Abby arrived. They went to the closet to hang up their coats. Madeline had noticed that Martin didn't stash his 'umbrella' in the closet anymore, but instead kept it on a shelf under the cash register. She was glad to know that both Martin's cudgel and Abby's gun were at the ready.

She walked over to Abby who said, "I've been meaning to ask you about Harley's watches. How many did he have?"

"Eleven, all 18-karat gold, including the bands."

"And how much are they worth?"

"In total? About one point four million dollars."

That got Abby's attention. Even Martin, pulling off his black snow boots, looked up.

"You're kidding. Why would anyone spend that kind of money on watches? That's crazy," said Abby.

"One of them is now worth at least four hundred thousand, probably more," Madeline announced. "Harley's father gave him a 24-karat gold Patek after a civil war in Algeria in 2002 was over. Chase didn't tell me that, I figured that out myself."

Martin laughed. "Harley must have done something spectacular," and Abby agreed.

Neither one was as impressed as Madeline thought they should be with her brilliant bit of detective work.

Madeline went to her desk. Well, at least she was impressed with herself, even if it didn't mean she was any closer to actually helping Olivia. Nevertheless, Madeline was feeling good that she'd solved that mystery. At last, she'd actually accomplished something, even if it was small. Maybe, just maybe she could still find some way to help Olivia, even if she had run out of people to talk to. Although she could always just talk to Olivia again. It wouldn't hurt to see her and go over old ground and see if anything popped up. It certainly couldn't hurt.

Madeline dialed Olivia's number.

* * *

"Hi Olivia," said Madeline when she picked up. We haven't talked for a while, and I thought I'd see how everything is going?"

"About the same. My lawyer is still working on getting the case against me dismissed, but I am staying optimistic. I'll just have to wait and see what happens."

"You know what, let's have dinner tonight and catch up."

"That's a nice idea," said Olivia. "How about if you come by my hotel around 6:00 tonight? I'm at the Four Seasons in the Back Bay. I know of a great restaurant in Quincy, so get dressed up. No sense both of us driving there either. Meet me here, and I'll drive to Quincy."

"That sounds perfect. I'll see you at six then. Have you been able to get back in your house yet?"

"Yes, at last. Well, I didn't go myself, I'll never set foot in that house again. I had movers pack up the rest of my clothes, Limoges dishes, and the silver, plus a couple of paintings Harley gave me. There was nothing else I wanted. Chase must have already been there because the movers told me when they arrived the place was pretty much empty. Edgar told me you'd had a meeting with him."

"I did," said Madeline." He's not much of a talker, is he?"

"No, he isn't, is he? By the way, Madeline, would you mind appraising my jewelry? I was thinking that is something I should have done."

"Yes, I can take care of that for you. We can talk about that tonight."

It wasn't lost on Madeline that Olivia seemed to have a continual string of things for her to do.

* * *

At her desk in her study, Madeline decided to move her two eBooks into her Harley folder on her desktop. She clicked on the Algeria eBook, but it opened instead, so she skimmed through it one last time, proud of her detective work in identifying the date on Harley's watch. This time she scrolled to the second section of four-color photos in the back, with the subtitle, "A Generation Gone," and a paragraph explaining that by 2002 the Algerians pictured in that section were all dead, killed during the brutal civil war. She scrolled through all these photos because these weren't pictures of death and blood, but rather, based on the captions, photos of prominent Algerians; generals, politicians, and wealthy owners of the country's oil and gas fields and refineries that were privately held. And all of them killed in the civil war.

The men were in suits and ties, except for several men in uniform with

160

rows of medals; the women mostly in evening gowns. Madeline had to smile, who wore evening gowns these days? She almost closed the book but kept on. One photo dated 1994, was of a glamorous woman in a brown cape, staring straight into the camera, her long, dark hair pulled back in a chignon. Her piercing eyes stared straight into the camera, an emerald necklace around her neck. The woman was in another photo, in profile this time. Madeline closed the eBook and dropped it in her Harley folder. The war had certainly been a tragedy.

* * *

Madeline went down in the garage for her car, wearing what was now her only suit, a rose-colored Burberry with a cinched waist, a blood-red scarf around her neck, and low heels. She headed to Olivia's hotel, checking her rearview mirror. She didn't think she was being followed until she was almost in the Back Bay and noticed a gray Toyota had been two cars behind her after four turns. But after she drove down a one-way street for three blocks and made two sudden right turns the car disappeared. It might not have even been following her anyway. At the hotel, the valet took her car and Madeline went up to Olivia's suite.

Olivia answered the door in a black cashmere dress with subtle silk embroidery of a pale green dragon running the length of her right sleeve. She was wearing her emeralds of course.

"You pulled out all the stops," said Madeline. "That's a beautiful dress."

"It is, isn't it? I had it custom-made right before I left Macau five years ago and moved to The Hague." She looked at Madeline. "That's in the Netherlands."

"Why there?"

"I had things I needed to do there. I was looking for something."

"Something?"

"Yes. It's a long, boring story." She looked Madeline up and down. "No cowboy boots tonight?"

"No, I don't wear cowboy boots all of the time, just almost all the time. It's a family thing."

Which was true. Madeline's adored older sister, Luella, had gone by the nickname 'Dude' from the time she was twelve, because she wore only cowboy boots, and couldn't be talked out of it. Dude had gone on to get a Ph.D. in Marine Biology, which still surprised their mother, Marian. She had always thought Dude would end up in prison.

* * *

Olivia led Madeline into the living room of her suite, where a bottle of white wine, glasses, and a tray of brie and crackers sat on the coffee table.

Olivia poured wine in both glasses, and picked up her glass. "I propose a toast to my lawyer. He needs it. He's still trying to get the charge against me dismissed. The only thing I can do is wait."

The two women clinked glasses, and they sat down.

"Do they have any new suspects?" asked Madeline.

"I have no idea."

Madeline proposed another toast. "Let's toast to finding new suspects," and they clinked glasses again.

Ten minutes later Olivia topped off her glass of wine, and Madeline's as well. When Olivia awkwardly picked up her glass, half of the chardonnay splashed on the embroidered dragon on her right sleeve and down the side of her dress. "Well, that was clumsy," said Olivia and stood up quickly, "I'll be back in just a minute. Have a look around, this is really a lovely suite."

Olivia walked around the corner and after a minute Madeline stood up. Yes, her suite was very elegant; smoke gray granite everywhere, pale green silk wallpaper on the walls, and dark gray leather furniture. She walked down a hall, the door to the master bathroom half-open. Olivia stood at the sink, the back of her dress unzipped, carefully dabbing a damp hand towel on the splashes of wine along the sleeve.

With a shock, Madeline saw that Olivia's entire back, from her waist to her neck, was crisscrossed with long, thick scars. Madeline quickly turned and walked back to the coffee table and their wine glasses.

162

Olivia returned to the living room several minutes later, brushing the side of her dress. "Anyway, I have almost given up hope that the police will ever find the man in brown. All I can do is hope for the best. Well, we should be going. I made reservations at The Tavern at Granite Links in Quincy. I think you'll like it."

Olivia pulled her hair back in a chignon, secured it with her emerald clip, and the two women went down to the lobby and out to Olivia's BMW.

Chapter Sixteen

The valet had Olivia's BMW waiting for them by the front door of the hotel. Madeline glanced around but didn't see an idling gray Toyota, so whoever had been following her had given up. Or maybe she hadn't been followed. Olivia tipped the valet as Madeline slid into the passenger seat, picking up an old camera on the floor. Olivia took it and tossed it on the back seat, and it rolled off on the floor with a thud.

"Don't worry," said Olivia, "it doesn't work anyway."

Madeline laughed, "Do you always drive around with a camera that doesn't work?"

Olivia's head snapped up and she glanced at Madeline but didn't say anything.

"Any news on Penelope's kayak accident?" asked Madeline.

"Not really. My lawyer heard she kept her kayak at her mother's place in Hull, in the Atlantic Hill ll building, the one they call The Pyramid at the head of Nantasket Beach. Unfortunately, so far no one had seen anyone messing with one of the kayaks stored there. Who knows how long that investigation will take? Forever maybe."

* * *

Olivia merged into I-93 South's heavy traffic, and said, "What have you been up to?"

"Up to? Believe it or not, I've been reading up on civil wars," said Madeline.

"Civil wars? Really? That's a dreary subject. Why?" asked Olivia.

"When I was appraising Harley's watches there was an inscription on the back of one of his Patek watches, with a date, in 2002."

Suddenly Olivia changed lanes, took a hair raising-exit, and after two miles jumped back on I-93. "Sorry, I had a tail I had to get rid of," she said nonchalantly, her eyes on the rearview mirror. "And I did."

Madeline looked out the back window, behind them was a long, snaking line of headlights.

Olivia glanced at Madeline. "I never noticed an inscription on any of Harley's watches, although I never looked. What did this one say?"

"Just congratulations for a good job or something."

"Harley had too many watches," said Olivia.

"There was a date too," said Madeline, "February 8, 2002. Which I'm convinced had something to do with the Algerian Civil War."

Olivia glanced over at Madeline. "You are? Really? I'm surprised you even know about that war, not many people do. The watch must have been from a client."

"No, the watch was a gift from his father, Daniel. Congratulating Harley for getting them out, or words to that effect." Madeline laughed. "It didn't say out of what."

"Harley had a thing about expensive watches," said Olivia with a laugh, "and expensive guns. He spent way too much money on both. So did his father, obviously."

Olivia's eyes were now constantly flickering between the dark road ahead and the rearview mirror. She said, "We'll be there in about ten or fifteen minutes. Too bad it's dark because the views from the restaurant are spectacular. Harley loved the place, I swear we had dinner there at least once a week."

"How did you meet Harley again?" Then she said, "Oh, I remember now, you were working on a paper, something about civilian populations."

"That's right, the title was *The Impact of Armed Conflict on Civilian Populations*. I had to sift through stacks and stacks of original source material to get any real information. It was easier at the UN since a lot of their material is digitized."

"Where was your paper published?"

"It was never published, I wasn't able to finish it. I will, though, someday. But Harley was very helpful. More helpful than he realized I think." Olivia smiled. She took off the scarf around her neck, and Madeline glanced at her profile bathed in moonlight, and then looked again. Olivia looked exactly like the striking-looking woman she'd just admired in the eBook photos of prominent Algerians. The same hawk nose, the same deep brown eyes, the same full lips. But it was the emerald necklace around Olivia's neck that did it.

"Olivia, you look exactly, and I mean exactly like a woman in a book I was just reading, on the Algerian Civil War." She had to glance at Olivia's profile again, the resemblance was uncanny. Olivia reached up and adjusted the pendant on her emerald necklace, and Madeline remembered what Olivia had said about the gold khit errouh her mother had given her.

"Olivia, I'm just curious, was your mother Algerian?"

Olivia turned to look at Madeline. "My mother? Don't be ridiculous. My mother was Tunisian. I grew up in Tunis, then I lived in Paris for years, Macau too, did I ever mention Macau? I was even at The Hague for a year. And then New York and Boston."

"Well, the woman who looks just like you was Algerian." Madeline continued. "The book said she was from a prominent family there. I think the name was D'Aragon."

"Never heard of the name," said Olivia abruptly, staring straight ahead, peering into the darkness. She didn't say anything further, but a mile later she took an abrupt left onto an old and narrow, road, "Hold on, it's a bit of a rough ride, but I want to show you the old Quincy Quarry first, which will only take a couple of minutes. It will be beautiful in the moonlight tonight, and we have time. The quarry is filled in now, but it's still quite a dramatic place."

A sliver of anxiety ran down Madeline's back. She glanced behind them, they were the only car on the road.

Olivia's hands were now clenched on the wheel, her face tight with concentration as she drove down the rutted road. Madeline noticed they hadn't passed any buildings much less houses on the isolated road, and the darkness was almost total. The only light was from the moon, which was intermittently masked by thick clouds moving in.

Madeline said, tense now, "You know what, I'm starving," as she looked out the window as dark, looming trees in the Blue Hills Reservation slowly flashed by. "Olivia, I don't want to go to look at an old quarry tonight, I really don't. Let's just go to the restaurant."

Olivia didn't look at her but continued driving down the narrow road for another mile and Madeline said in the uneasy silence, "Olivia, I said I really don't want to go to the quarry."

Olivia jammed her foot on the accelerator and the speedometer inched up to 35 mph on the old road.

"I think you should see it." She turned to Madeline, her face pale and cold in a sudden ray of moonlight. "Just relax, it will be worth it. Besides, we're almost there."

Madeline looked at Olivia again. She thought about the inscription on Harley's Patek watch and said, keeping her voice casual, "Olivia, was Harley in Algeria years ago? He was, wasn't he?"

Olivia must have pressed a control by the steering wheel because Madeline thought she heard a lock click on the passenger door. There was no expression on Olivia's face as she abruptly turned onto an even narrower dirt road, barely slowing and Madeline tried the handle on her door. It was locked.

"What is going on for God's sake? What are you doing?" said Madeline, her voice flat. "Turn the car around now!"

Olivia ignored her and continued driving down the old dark road, heavy clouds totally masking the moon now, even the sound of the tires on the gravel was menacing. And then Olivia accelerated yet again.

Madeline knew then there was only one thing she could do, and it was now or never. She leaned over and with her left hand grabbed the steering wheel and yanked it hard to the left. The car veered up an embankment, bucked, and then stalled, the motor whining.

* * *

Olivia reached a hand under her seat, and when she yanked it out, she had a gun in her hand.

"Step out of the car. Now," Olivia demanded, and Madeline heard another click as her door was unlocked. But Madeline didn't check her door again, nor did she bother to look at Olivia.

Instead, she grabbed for the gun and the two women struggled, but Madeline had a stronger grip on the weapon and she wrenched it from Olivia's hand. Olivia lunged for the pistol and it fired with an enormous boom inside the car, the bullet striking Madeline in the thigh. She shuddered once and fell back against the seat. The thick smell of burnt gunpowder filled the car, hanging in the air.

Holding the gun by the warm muzzle, Madeline swung back her right hand and struck Olivia as hard as she could on the temple with the gun butt. Olivia crumpled against the steering wheel and Madeline leaned across her, pushed the driver's side door open, and shoved Olivia out of the car to the ground and she lay still.

Madeline clambered out, the gun in her right hand, and barely able to stand, she stepped over Olivia. Madeline leaned against the car, pulled out her cell phone with her left hand, and punched 911 with her thumb.

The operator asked, "What's your emergency?"

"I'm in the Blue Hills and I've been shot. I have the gun in my hand. A woman I know pulled it on me and there was a struggle and I got shot. I knocked her out with the gun, and she's on the ground." A pause as Madeline listened, then said, "No, it was just the two of us in the car. Please send the police and an ambulance right away." She was breathing now in short gasps because of the stabbing pain in her thigh. "You have my location?"

"Yes, from your phone. Where is the gun now?"

"In my hand."

"I'm sending help now. Give me your name and tell me what happened."

Madeline told the woman her name and said "I'm not really sure what happened..." and Madeline suddenly all but doubled over as bolts of pain from the bullet in her thigh shot down her leg.

Olivia tried to get to her feet and Madeline dropped her phone in her jacket pocket, "Olivia, if you move one more time, I'll shoot you, I will," said Madeline. "There was no man in brown, was there? You made that up. You shot Harley."

Olivia looked up at Madeline, her brown eyes flashing. "Go to hell." Olivia tried to get to her feet again and Madeline wondered if there were any more bullets left in the cartridge.

"I said don't move, or I'll shoot you," and Olivia slumped back down to the ground. Good, so there must still be at least one bullet in the cartridge.

Madeline looked down at the heavy pistol, but she didn't want to set it on the ground. She put both hands on the gun, "You murdered Harley, didn't you Olivia? There was no man in brown. You shot him."

Oliva only stared over her head into the trees. Madeline leaned against the car as she waited for the police and an ambulance, her eyes never leaving Olivia. Madeline noticed fresh blood on the leaves on the ground, which could be hers. She checked her thigh, a river of blood was running down her leg. She set the gun down, grabbed the scarf around her neck, and tied a quick tourniquet above the bullet wound as best as she could. Olivia hadn't moved. Madeline was breathing harshly from the pain, but the tourniquet must have been tight enough because the bleeding stopped. Her cell phone rang, but she let it ring. She picked up the gun.

* * *

Madeline heard the wail of sirens several minutes later. She watched as two ambulances and three police cars pulled up beside Olivia's car, still stalled on the embankment. A cop jumped out of the lead squad car, gun drawn, and ran up to her. She handed the cop Olivia's gun and he motioned to the EMT's inside the ambulances, and they came running.

The officer said, "Are you Madeline Lane?"

"Yes," said Madeline. Olivia was on a stretcher in less than a minute, and was wheeled to the ambulance, a bloody bandage around her head. Madeline said to the cop, "She pulled a gun on me in the car, and I got it away from her but it fired when she tried to grab it. That's how I got shot. So I hit her with the gun butt." A minute later Madeline too was strapped on a stretcher, and she lost consciousness.

Later, she wasn't sure how much later, Madeline vaguely remembered talking to the police under the fluorescent glare of an ER exam room. She did tell them Olivia had pulled a gun on her, but other than that, Madeline was pretty sure she just rambled about Harley. Then she lost consciousness again.

* * *

When Madeline woke up it took her a couple of seconds to realize she was in a narrow bed with railings. A hospital bed. She put her hand tentatively on her left thigh. All she felt was bandages, but no pain.

A familiar voice said, "Your leg is still there. I looked."

She glanced up. Abby was standing by her bed and she said, "What a horrible, god-awful night you've had Madeline. Olivia is here, in the hospital, but in police custody." Madeline didn't say anything, and Abby continued, "How do you feel?"

"Bad, I feel very, very bad. Olivia murdered Harley, she shot him. It was her. I didn't want to believe it, but now I do."

"Olivia had a gun with her tonight?"

"Yes, she had a gun under the seat of her car."

"Well, all I can say is thank God you're alive. The doctor said you'll be fine."

"Good, I suppose. How is Olivia?"

"I was told she has a concussion. A bad one."

"Olivia was the one who murdered Harley," she repeated. "It was her."

"I am sorry, Madeline. You were convinced she was innocent," said Abby.

"Yes, I was. I believed her, I really did. I wanted to believe her. She saved my life you know, and then, in the car tonight she pulled a gun on me and..."

Madeline tried to sit up, but she sank back down on the bed and closed her eyes.

* * *

Two uniformed policemen walked in then, and Abby said to her, "After you're discharged from the hospital you'll be staying at my place for a few days. Call me tonight though, no matter what time, if you can't sleep... I'll be back tomorrow and take you to my place."

Abby kissed her on the cheek and left.

The cops told her they knew Olivia had been charged with second-degree murder in Harley's death and had been out on bail.

"Her bail has now been revoked, of course," said one of the cops. "How did you know Mrs. Atherton?"

Madeline explained how she knew her, telling them that although she didn't witness the shooting she had been on Harley's patio less than a minute after he'd been shot.

"Tell us why she pulled a gun on you tonight?"

A tricky question she knew they'd ask. She had already decided she would not go into a long story of old photographs of a dead mother, or of a tragic civil war. There was too much she didn't know, so the less said, the better.

"I was talking about the afternoon Harley was shot and it made her angry I guess," began Madeline.

She stopped and Madeline looked at the officers, waiting for her to continue. Madeline reached for a bottle of water on the bedside tray, took a long drink, and said, "Olivia insisted we go see the old Quincy Quarry on our way to dinner, and then she locked my door and I grabbed the wheel and we stalled on an embankment and she pulled out a gun. I grabbed the gun from her and then boom, I got shot, so I hit her with the gun on the side of her head. I don't know what she was thinking."

She must have nodded off because when she opened her eyes the police were gone.

Five minutes later a tall, thin and tired doctor in his mid-forties walked in, introduced himself as the surgeon, and examined the wound on her thigh.

He sighed, "It was a little tricky, but the bullet was successfully removed. The good news is it just missed a bone, and there is minimal muscle tear so you should completely recover. I'll come by tomorrow morning to check the stitches, and there's a good chance you can be released right after. You won't need crutches, but just take it easy and maybe use a cane for a couple of days."

* * *

When Madeline woke up again it was after 1:00 am but she had trouble falling back asleep. She thought about the drive that night with Olivia, a drive that had turned into a nightmare when she brought up the inscription on Harley's watch. She had so wanted to believe that Olivia had simply been in the wrong place at the wrong time when Harley had been murdered. But that wasn't true.

She wanted to talk to Felix, and she stared at her phone. She'd call him at 5:30 am, just a couple of hours away. After all, the man got up at 5:30 am every damn day.

* * *

Madeline barely slept the rest of that night because she couldn't stop thinking about Olivia. She had no doubt now that once they would have arrived at the Quincy Quarry there would have been an 'accident' of some kind, and she would have been dead. Olivia had used her to get information on the police investigation, but then Madeline had stumbled on the truth, or part of the truth anyway. And Olivia wanted her dead. Madeline didn't know what the whole truth was. Yet.

Madeline finally got out of bed carefully, her leg throbbing, and hobbled to the bathroom with a cane. She looked in the mirror of her hospital room. She looked a wreck, her short blonde hair was, and she leaned closer to the mirror, actually sticking out sideways. She glanced at her watch; it was 5:45 and Felix would be showered and shaved by now, and about to have his first cup of coffee.

However, in the cold light of a cold morning, she decided not to call him.

It was better to just let it go.

* * *

Just after 8:30 am, the two policemen came back to talk to Madeline in her hospital room.

One of them said, "Olivia hasn't spoken a word since she was brought into the hospital. Not a single, solitary word. When we ask her a question, she doesn't even look at us. She just lies in her bed, with no emotion on her face, staring at the ceiling. She ate breakfast and appears to be able to hear, but she's not speaking. Her lawyer is with her now."

"Does she have any family?" the officer asked.

"No, she told me everyone in her family is dead."

"Everyone?"

"She told me she had no family."

"The doctor," said one of the policemen, "told us her entire back is covered with old burn scars. Do you know anything about that? We're asking only in case it might have a bearing on our investigation."

"Old scars? I caught a glimpse of them yesterday at her hotel, but I have no idea how she got them. I didn't ask her."

They went over her statement from the night before. "Unless you have anything else to add, we'll have a final statement for you to sign before you leave the hospital," said the lead officer. They both thanked her and left.

Chapter Seventeen

Three hours later, Madeline was discharged. Abby came to pick her up. She handed Madeline a bouquet of purple hyacinths from Martin.

"He said he couldn't resist because they match your new cowboy boots. God forbid, you have purple ones now?"

"Wasn't that sweet? But my boots are lavender, not purple. My sister Dude would approve, although she'd have gone with purple. Speaking of which, she just got a twelve-month contract on the Cape, at the Woods Hole Oceanographic Institute."

"I thought she was in Moscow?"

"No, she got..." Madeline almost said "thrown out of the country." Instead she said, "...tired of it."

Abby drove Madeline to her house in Cambridge, a silent ride since Madeline told Abby she didn't want to talk about Olivia. Twenty minutes later she was settled in the living room in a big recliner that had belonged to Abby's husband, with her left leg up, a tall glass of orange juice, two bagels with cream cheese, and the TV remote on a tray beside her. Her hyacinths from Martin were beside her, in a vase.

"Call me if you need anything else," said Abby.

"Thanks, the only things I can think of are a joint and a martini."

Abby just smiled and walked out the door.

* * *

Alone now, Madeline blindly stared out the living room window at the park across the street, thinking about Olivia. She recalled a couple of times when Harley had been on his cell phone, he'd been angry that he wasn't getting the information he'd been expecting. She remembered that both times Olivia had paid close attention to the call, and she had been nervous, anxious even as she listened to his side of the conversation. So, Olivia had known something was up.

Madeline wanted to know what that was.

Felix had told her he'd done some digging into Harley's background, and that both Harley and his father had been investigated for war crimes by the International Criminal Court. Now that she thought about it that was the same organization where Olivia said she had worked at as a researcher. That could be a coincidence, but she didn't think so. What was the name of that small town in Algeria where Felix had said there'd been an explosion and the whole town burned to the ground? She couldn't remember, and finally, she did, El-Traynor.

She called Abby. "I'm fine, but could you please give Martin a key to my place in my desk drawer and ask him if he could stop by and pick up my laptop and charger and bring it to me here? It's important, or I wouldn't ask."

Abby, God bless her, didn't press Madeline for an explanation.

An hour later Martin dropped off her laptop, and she thanked him, and for the flowers. As soon as he left she went into her Algeria eBook and checked the index, and there it was, 'The El-Traynor Annihilation.' Which sounded horrible, and it was.

The article mentioned the very wealthy Algerian family, the D'Aragons, who owned several large oil fields and refineries in El-Traynor that were bombed in 2001 in an air attack toward the end of their civil war. The bombs destroyed the oil wells and refineries, but there had been a massive firestorm that spread to the nearby village and ignited a warehouse that stored several thousand tons of the fertilizer, ammonium nitrate. There was a huge explosion and the entire town was destroyed in the inferno. Over 2,000 civilians had died.

The rich owners, the D'Aragons, also perished, and their 24-year-old daughter, a doctor, who was a surgical resident at a hospital in Algiers, was presumed dead, her body never recovered.

The bombing of a civilian target and the significant death toll caused outrage not just in Algeria but across all of North Africa. After the war three separate tribunals had been convened by the Algerian government that sought to establish responsibility for the now-infamous "El-Traynor Annihilation." However, they were disbanded without a determination of blame. And later, while the International Criminal Court did investigate several individuals, which the article didn't name, no actual charges were ever brought by the ICC due to lack of evidence.

Madeline stretched out on the recliner. The pieces were coming together, but there were parts still missing. Olivia was definitely the daughter of the wealthy D'Aragon family, and an explosion and massive fire would explain a lot of things. Olivia must have decided she had to permanently silence Madeline the night before once she'd mentioned the D'Aragon name. It was right after that that Olivia had turned off the road, to the Quincy Quarry.

* * *

Madeline pulled out her cell phone and called Edgar. Since he was a man of few words Madeline got right to the point.

"I need to see you. I just got out of the hospital. Olivia pulled a gun on me last night."

She listened for a moment and then said, "Yes, that's right, a gun. I ended up getting shot and she ended up with a concussion. She is in police custody at Massachusetts General for now. I'm at my partner Abby's place in Cambridge."

Madeline listened for a moment, then said to him, "In an hour? Yes, that would be good," and she gave him Abby's address.

Exactly an hour later the doorbell rang, and she grabbed her cane, limped to the hall, and opened the door.

Edgar walked in and actually smiled when he saw her. It was the first time she'd ever seen the man smile. She led him to the living room, and he sat by her recliner.

"Details please," he said.

"First of all," she began, "Olivia murdered Harley," and Madeline told him the whole story of her drive the evening before with Olivia, his eyes never leaving her face, mentioning Olivia's mother this time in her story. And then she gave him the information about the bombing mission in Algeria's El-Traynor, that she now believed Harley had ordered.

Edgar said, "And you wanted to see me because—"

"There are some things about Olivia that I think you know. I'm guessing Harley had you or someone else run a background check on Olivia before they were married. For one thing, I know Olivia was Algerian."

Edgar hesitated, and then began, "Harley definitely did not know that Olivia was Algerian. I am positive he did not know that. According to her passport, she is Tunisian, born in Tunis. Harley had me run a background check on her before they were married, and Olivia's life was pretty straightforward. She was born in Tunis, graduated from the university, lived in Paris for a couple of years, married a Portuguese importer, and they moved to Macau. She divorced him five years ago and moved to The Hague, where she worked in the International Criminal Court's research department, and then to New York City, and worked the UN, getting a job in research again, and then she met Harley. That's about it."

"How much of it is true?"

He shrugged. "I'm not sure, most of it probably. Or, let me say, it all checked out."

"But Harley was suspicious?"

"I would say he became suspicious."

"Why?"

"Harley told me Olivia's entire back is covered with thick scars from her waist to her shoulders. She'd told him she almost died in a very bad car accident in Tunis years ago when she was in her twenties and was in a hospital there for months. He also told me when he had someone check her story, no records of that accident or hospital stay were ever found, anywhere. He asked her about that, and she told him the records must have been just misplaced or lost."

"I've seen her scars," said Madeline. "Well, I caught a glimpse of them. They were horrific."

"I also ran another check on both of her passports as well as her birth certificate for Harley three weeks ago," said Edgar, "and they are definitely not forgeries. If what you are telling me is true, Olivia must have assumed the identity of a woman from Tunisia who died years ago. And I suspect Harley may have thought that as well. That could have been what he was trying to verify before he was murdered, and why he flew to Paris. I noticed a couple of little things myself. Like she didn't know that the A4 is the link with Bizerte in Tunis, which anyone who lived there would have known."

"Why do you know that?"

He shrugged.

"But Edgar, assuming that Olivia was injured in the air attack and the explosion in El-Traynor, why would she need a new identity?"

"I don't know what her parents' or even Olivia's politics were, or which side they were on in the civil war, but she was obviously afraid for her life. There was a big National Reconciliation in Algeria after the civil war, and an amnesty law was passed, but not until 2006. She was living in Macau by then." He shrugged and continued, "I know how Harley thinks; it seems to me now, he must have been trying to find out *who she wasn't*. Which I am guessing he did find out. Once he knew that, then he would have set out to find out *who she was*." Edgar sat perfectly still on the sofa. "Unfortunately, he didn't have that chance."

Madeline didn't say anything, she just stared at him.

"Harley was quite devoted to Olivia, you know, until he began to suspect that she wasn't who she said she was."

Madeline's thigh began to throb, and she shifted in the chair. "Edgar, what was in the files from Wallace's time that Chase has? Look, I have to know. Can you tell me what was in them?"

Edgar ran his hand over his face and stared at the floor, then up at Madeline. She continued, "I need you to tell me. Please."

"Harley never directly told me what happened in Algeria, but over the last couple of years I picked up bits and pieces from him. And then I did go through Wallace's files a couple of days ago, but they were incomplete. Harley did order the bombing of a couple of oil refineries and wells, in Algeria years ago. In a town called El-Traynor. I'm double checking on who owned them, but I'm pretty sure they were owned by the D'Aragon family, and—"

"I think…"

"Let me finish. The bombing of El-Traynor didn't go as planned. It was to be a 'precision' attack, on the outskirts of the little town. Algeria was a mess back then, and a month or so before the bombing Wallace wanted Harley to completely pull Atherton Global's contractors and equipment out of Algeria, but Harley wanted one last, well-paying mission. So, he set up an airstrike, and the oil wells and the refineries were totally destroyed. But the fires got out of control, and a warehouse exploded in the village, and the town was all but obliterated. There was a huge backlash because a couple of thousand civilians died, with both sides in the war denying responsibility. The ironic thing is that it actually did spur the end of that war. Two months later peace talks began, and Atherton Global was able to get out of Algeria with its reputation, its equipment, and its teams all intact."

"That's why Harley's dad gave him an incredibly valuable watch?"

"I don't know anything about Harley's father much less about a valuable watch. There was an investigation of the 'El-Traynor Annihilation' as it came to be known, but it was never proved what group was behind the bombing. Anyway, that information was there in Wallace's file."

"Which Chase now has."

"Had. It had information Chase didn't need to know. I went into his place while he was at work and took them."

"What do you mean you 'went into'?"

"I disarmed all the alarms, sensors, and cameras, walked in the back door, found the files, and took them."

"Where were they? I tried to find them."

Edgar gave her a sharp look and continued, "After I read them, I shredded every last page. If it ever came out which side was responsible, even now, even after the big 'reconciliation' there would be calls for revenge and a lot of bloodshed, and the whole mess could erupt into a new war."

"That's what you meant when you said 'political dynamite'?"

"Yes, so I got rid of the evidence. End of story."

"Edgar, who did Harley think Olivia was?"

"Towards the end, he wasn't sure who she was. Harley had become obsessed with conspiracies these last six months, and the thought that Olivia might not be who she said she was, made him worse. There, I've told you everything I know. I have nothing more for you." He stood up.

Madeline said, "Edgar, did you have someone following me?"

"Only for a day." Edgar smiled and left.

* * *

Madeline sat in Abby's living room thinking about Olivia, a woman with an all-consuming rage and an inflexible determination, and also a woman who was undeniably capable of murder. More than one, she thought. She heard footsteps on Abby's porch and the doorbell rang. She opened the door and Donia walked in.

"I went to the store and Abby said you were here. I have to talk to you."

"Of course, come in."

"She told me that Olivia was the one who murdered Harley. And that last night you got shot, by Olivia."

"That's not exactly correct. Technically I shot myself since the gun was in my hand. But your point is well taken."

Donia almost smiled and then she said, "I wanted you to know before you just heard it on the news..." She stopped.

"Know what?"

"Almost an hour ago Olivia was scheduled to be moved from Massachusetts General to a prison medical unit at MCI-Framingham, handcuffed but not shackled. Then, while she was being transferred to the police ambulance, she was able to knock down one of the officers and get his gun. She had it aimed at his head when his partner shot and killed her. Olivia is dead, Madeline, and it's about to be all over the news."

Madeline stood stock still, and the color drained from her face. "What? She's dead? Olivia is dead?" Donia nodded, and Madeline turned and led her to the living room.

"Yes. She is dead, she died instantaneously."

Tears sprang into Madeline's eyes. "I can't believe it, I just can't believe it. Why would Olivia do that? She had to know she couldn't escape, she had to know that."

Donia sighed. "She probably did, at least on some level. When all was said and done, what with all the charges she was facing, she would likely have ended up with a twenty-five or thirty-year prison sentence. Or a life sentence with no chance of parole if the prosecutor decided to move forward with a first-degree murder charge in Harley's case."

Madeline told her about the car ride with Olivia, the edited version, the one she'd given the police, with no mention of Algeria, or Olivia's mother. Much less her real name.

"I am sorry," said Donia, "I know that you were trying to help her."

"I believed Olivia, I totally believed her, and I wanted to help her. She was always asking me for information about the investigation into Harley's murder, which I gladly provided. I was useful to Olivia, for a while, until I wasn't. Still, I never thought she was capable of even one murder, much less a couple of them."

"What do mean a couple of murders?" said Donia, giving her a sharp look. "She committed a couple of murders?"

"Oh, sorry, I'm just in shock. Don't pay attention to anything I say." Madeline had momentarily forgotten that Donia was an ex-homicide cop, and tenacious in the extreme. The two women talked about Olivia and her escape attempt for half an hour and then Donia left.

Madeline limped back to her recliner. She was pretty certain now that Olivia had been responsible for Penelope's death too, who had not so subtly hinted when Madeline had been in her condo that Olivia might not be who she said she was. Was Olivia capable of drilling a hole in Penelope's kayak and then patching it so it would sink in rough weather to keep her secret safe? Absolutely.

Perhaps Olivia had murdered Wallace too. He could have seen photos of Olivia during the extensive media coverage of the 'El-Traynor Annihilation' when he'd been in Algeria with Harley. Penelope had told Madeline that less than two weeks ago Wallace had wanted to talk to her about a photo of someone he'd just seen who he thought had been dead for years. That certainly could have been Olivia. Then too, the day that Wallace had been murdered in New Hampshire, had Olivia been the woman with a camera that a witness spotted in that area? Yes, Olivia was capable of murdering Wallace to stop him from talking.

Still, there was nothing Madeline could do. There was just no hard evidence in either case that their deaths had been anything other than accidental. Which didn't ultimately matter, because Olivia was dead now too. Justice had been served and delivered with finality, just not in the usual way.

As for Harley, it seemed that Olivia had spent the last couple of years tracking down the name of the person who had ordered the bombing of El Traynor, and she had had to search through layers of old field research at the ICC in the Netherlands and the UN in New York for that information. And that must have been how she learned that Harley A. Atherton of Atherton Global Security had been behind the bombing.

Madeline had no doubt Harley's death warrant was as good as signed the moment Olivia learned his name, because she did track him down, and she made sure she met him. The marriage? That was likely a way to replace her lost inheritance once he was dead. She probably had not intended to kill him so soon, but once Harley knew her Tunisian identity was false, she would have had to.

How much should Madeline tell of this story? She knew that laying bare the truth behind the El-Traynor Annihilation would serve no real purpose, it would just burst open and inflame an old, sad wound. So Madeline would say nothing about Harley's involvement in the bombing and the catastrophic fires of El-Traynor to anyone. Maybe someday, in calmer times, the whole story would see the light of day, but it wasn't up to her to see that it did.

Madeline sighed and looked down at her computer as a wave of crushing loneliness swept over her. She wanted to be with someone because there was just too much sadness and death, too many tragic secrets to deal with alone. She pulled out her phone and called Felix.

He answered saying, "I heard the news about Olivia. I am so sorry."

"Felix, could you come and be with me? I'm at Abby's right now, and I would like your arms around me for a little while. Please."

Silence, and then he said, "I will be there in twenty minutes," and he hung up.

* * *

The investigation into Penelope's death was actively worked for six months, but there was no hard evidence that an actual crime had been committed, so it was finally closed as an accidental drowning. Wallace's shooting by a person or persons unknown did remain an open case, but it was no longer actively worked by the New Hampshire state police.

Olivia's true identity was never revealed either, and Madeline read in *The Globe* that Chase had her body shipped to France for burial in a cemetery in Paris. At first blush, that was a kind gesture, but it probably wasn't. Most likely Chase just wanted her far away from him. For forever. As for Edgar, she heard he had been fired from Atherton Global, and out of curiosity she tried to find out where he went, but no one at Atherton would say until the receptionist let it slip that Edgar was in Hong Kong, but no one knew who he was working for.

Madeline doubted she would ever learn exactly what Olivia had done in Algeria during their civil war, but she suspected Olivia had been very involved. But by the time the war was over, Olivia had lost everything. her family, as well as her fortune, and she was left with only a network of terrible burn scars on her body. She had obviously tried to make a new life, but that hadn't been enough, so she had gone on the hunt for revenge. As an employee, Olivia would have had access to both the ICC's and the UN's original field research, but Madeline didn't believe she'd gone to work for either to do research for some purported academic paper. Olivia was looking for a name in those old records, and she found it. Harley A. Atherton.

It seemed that Harley had learned Olivia's Tunisian identity was fake in Milton that afternoon after Madeline had dropped off the emerald necklace, in the phone call he'd been waiting for. He must have confronted Olivia with that information on the patio, and desperate, she would have pulled out a gun she'd taken from Harley's gun room, or grabbed one he could have set down on the coffee table, Madeline didn't know which, took aim, and pulled the trigger. And then, like a reverse *deus ex machina*, a minute later Madeline had walked around the corner while Olivia still had the weapon in her hand. Which left Olivia with no choice but to try and bluff her way out of Harley's murder.

It had almost worked.

The story of Olivia's dramatic and ultimately fatal attempt to escape from custody at Massachusetts General Hospital made the front page of *The Globe* for a week and was a story of interest for months afterwards. Madeline and Felix saw or spoke to each other every day during that time and they talked for hours. Sometimes she would whistle the French national anthem, and it never failed to make him laugh out loud.

* * *

Coda Gems had their best Holiday season so far that year, and their ruby promotion brought in a crush of new customers. Martin stayed on at the store after the Holidays, now permanently working three days a week. He of course brought his 'umbrella' with him to the store every day.

He also taught Madeline how to foxtrot, correctly.

Madeline did finally receive her concealed carry license, but she never did buy a gun. The smell of burnt gun powder now made her nauseous.

Acknowledgements

I am indebted to brilliant author and writing instructor Mary Buckham, to Susan Speakman who knows everything worth knowing, to Level Best Books publishers and editors, Verena Rose, Shawn Reilly Simmons, and Harriette Sackler, and their dedication to the art of crime fiction, to Jon Talbot for his killer ad designs, and finally to my oldest friend, Mary Adams, and her laser-sharp perception. Besides, she thinks I am funny.

About the Author

Mary E. Stibal has never considered 'less is more' a virtue, especially when it comes to gems. (Think Mrs. Simpson.) Mary has also long known that beautiful gems are a stone-cold motive for any manner of crime. Especially murder. So using her decades-long business background, Mary weaves stories of the deadly confluence of Boston's super-rich and their breathtaking jewels with blinding ambition and murder into a new series, "The Gemstone Mysteries." *A Widow in Pearls* is the first book in the series, with *An Ex-Heiress in Emeralds* its sequel. The third book, *A Sister in Rubies*, will be released in 2022.

CPSIA information can be obtained
at www.ICGtesting.com
Printed in the USA
LVHW021347180921
698156LV00005B/68